Intriguing Stories for the 21St Century

To Make You Laugh, Cry and Think

Dr. John Persico, Jr.

Edited by Ms. Socorro Luna

Table of Contents

Acknowledgements   1

Preface   3

The Stubborn Swedish Cow 5

The Mean Old Man and the Single Chair   8

The Story of the Lost Frederic Treasure   14

Ed, the Soldier   23

The Fox and the Rabbit   28

It's Coming Quick. It's Coming Quick. The End is Coming Quick   33

The Man Who Was Smarter than God   38

Four Young Boys Growing Up in America   46

Jesus: An Untold Story   58

A Day in the Life of a Hummingbird 62

The Bar Room Bum   67

Leandra   74

The Little Boy Who Believed in God   78

Autobiographies from the Dead – Cindy the Wife   81

Crying 84

A Conversation between Satan and God   86

Emily and Robert: A Love Story   94

The True Story of the Three Little Pigs: Well, Not So Little!   98

Alexa, I Need a Date for Saturday Night!   107

Tommy, A Boy for All Seasons   111

Samson and Delilah: A Modern Fable   117

Irony, Paradox, and Serendipity or Why a Donkey Knew Best!   122

Buddha and the Duck 126

Muhammed and the Christian Money Lender   130

A Simple Man Meets Faust   134

The Window   142

Perspiration or Inspiration: Which Is More Important to the Writer?   147

THE END   152

Acknowledgements

Here is where I get to recognize the people who have helped or nurtured my writing over the years leading up to this book. First, I thank my wife Karen for reading and commenting on so many of the stories I have written. Every author needs a fan base or even just a fan. Karen has been a wonderful fan.

I want to thank my editor Ms. Socorro Galusha. She is a diligent and inspired editor. She has reviewed every one of my stories and made many punctuation and grammatical changes. She has also suggested many content changes that have helped these stories with a better flow and overall meaning. She is a great friend and a great editor.

I want to thank my main muse Dr. Carolyn Wedin. Over the years, I have taken several writing classes with Dr. Wedin. She is truly a remarkable writer and inspiration. Carolyn inspires with praise and good ideas and not with criticism or fault finding. Her classes have led to many of her students publishing their own stories and books. If every student of writing had a teacher like Dr. Wedin, there would be many more great stories published.

I would be remiss if I did not mention the 101 great authors who have taught me much over the years. However, I think it would really be a bore for you to wade through my list. I will mention just five of my favorite authors: Mark Twain, Kurt Vonnegut, Dostoyevsky, Anatole France, and John Gardner. I think writers take a little bit of every author they read into their own writings. No one writes in a vacuum and I am grateful to the great writers who have left their mark on my desires.

Finally, I want to thank the many readers of my blog at www.agingcapriciously.com/. The hundreds of positive comments I have received over the years continue to motivate me to find new ideas and new subjects to share with others.

Preface

I have found four possible reasons for writing a book. One is to establish a professional standing. Academicians must publish or perish. Politicians and salespeople may write a book to gain prestige, fame, or status. A second reason for writing is simply mercenary. One may write in the hopes of making money. All authors would like to make money, but for some it is a primary reason. Getting a book on the "best seller's list" can seem like an easy road to fame and fortune. Alas, most writers will soon learn that it is anything but a fast path. A third reason is because you really believe that you have some knowledge or information that you want to share with people. You believe that your information will help people lead a better or more interesting life. Many self-help books, spiritual books and non-fiction books fit into this category.

The fourth reason deals with the simple joy of writing for writing sake alone. Authors like artists and musicians may be motivated because of the joy of the craft. Writing poses an endless possibility for regarding our own lives and the lives of others. There is no limit to the creativity that a writer can bring to the process of writing. This can be a double-edged sword. Sometimes the muse of creativity helps us to write prolifically and magnificently. Other times, the muse seems to desert us, and we find our landscape for writing to be barren and fruitless. Times like these can drive one to desperate straits.

The book you are holding is composed of stories I have written, "just for the fun of it." I have no dreams of becoming rich and famous with this book. It would be nice, but it is not likely. Many of these stories were tales I told on my blogsite over the past 10 or more years. Most of my blogs deal with non-fiction but every so often I have been moved to write something that seemed to be an exercise for me in creativity. Several of these stories stem from a bit of whimsy or to paraphrase Scrooge in Dicken's <u>The Christmas Carol</u>, my ideas may have come from "an undigested bit of beef, a blot of mustard, a crumb of cheese, a fragment of underdone potato."

I will admit that my most beloved stories when I was young came from Mark Twain, Uncle Remus, and Aesop. I loved fairy tales as well. My stories reflect a love for tales with morality and ethics. Life can be given meaning by blending fun, creativity and morality. I hope I have accomplished this with at least a few of my stories.

The Stubborn Swedish Cow

Introduction

The following story was written for my "Write-Now" class which was conducted by Dr. Carolyn Wedin, a retired professor emeritus from the University of Wisconsin. Dr. Wedin gave us a short email message she had received from a friend in Sweden about a cow who would not give milk. The assignment for the class was to use any element or perspective from the email to write a story. My story loosely embraces some of the key elements from the email, but is, of course embellished by my own writing fancies and imagination. Since I generally write social and political commentary, this story might seem a bit odd. However, if you reflect on it a while after you read it, I think you will find that there is a message or at least a few morals from this tale that you can take away.

The Stubborn Swedish Cow

Once upon a time there was an old farmer and his wife who had a cow that suddenly decided to stop giving milk. It was a Swedish cow, and you know how stubborn those Swedes can be. The old farmer was going to go out to talk to the cow but quite unexpectedly he choked to death on a bone in a piece of lutefisk. His wife now inherited the farm, the chickens, the pigs, and the stubborn Swedish cow who would not give any milk.

The farmer's wife went out to talk to the stubborn Swedish cow and tried to explain that without any milk, she would not be able to keep the farm and would have to sell everything. The chickens would go to Kentucky Fried Chicken and become original crispy chicken legs. The pigs would go to Famous Dave's

Barbecue and become hot and spicy pork ribs. Last but not least, she declared
that the stubborn Swedish cow would go to McDonald's where she would
probably become a Big Mc Double Cheeseburger Sandwich.

But the stubborn Swedish cow would not budge.

"I am tired of giving milk she thought to herself"

Being a stubborn Swedish cow she was not moved by the farmer's wife
arguments. However, the chickens and pigs heard all of the arguments and were
quite perturbed. The chickens nominated one of their own to go and talk to the
cow. "How selfish of you and inconsiderate," the delegated chicken
argued. "You don't care that we will become fried chicken; all you can think
about is yourself." This line of attack did not persuade the stubborn Swedish cow.

Next, the pigs decided to have a talk with the cow. In mass they went to see the
cow as pigs like to do everything together. In one voice, they pleaded with the
stubborn Swedish cow: "Please don't let us become barbecue ribs at Famous
Dave's we don't want to die. We know you have your reasons, but we hope you
will change your mind and save us all. You may be a stubborn Swedish cow, but
deep down inside you are really a good bovine." This line of swine reasoning
also failed to persuade the stubborn Swedish cow.

Unbeknownst to all, there was a small little field mouse that lived with his family
in the great barn. The field mouse had overheard the plight of the farmer's wife
and the arguments of the farm animals and was quite moved by their
problem. The field mouse was an avid reader and many of his kind would have
called him an intellectual. He was a follower of the famous Swedish philosopher

Emanuel Swedenborg. More recently he had read the Swedish philosopher Nick Bostrom well known for his work on existential risk, the Anthropic Principle, human enhancement ethics, superintelligence, the reversal test, and consequentialism.

The little field mouse decided to try explaining the theory of the Anthropic Principle to the cow in the hope that logic would prevail where pure emotion had failed.

"Listen please" said the little field mouse to the stubborn Swedish cow "The **Anthropic Principle** is the philosophical consideration that observations of the universe must be compatible with the conscious and sapient life that observes it. It is well known that cows give milk and to be a conscious cow, you have the obligation to perform this duty for the universe."

Now the cow had recently been reading from the writings of Dr. Niklas Boström and was quite impressed with this line of thought. "Yes", reflected the cow, "even though I am a stubborn Swede, I am also a creature of the universe with an infinite obligation to take my proper place in the grand scheme of things."

"You have convinced me" said the once stubborn Swedish cow to the little field mouse. "Hence forth, I will take my rightful place in the universe and give milk every day as long as I am able, thus fulfilling my role in the grand scheme of things"

And the farmer's wife, the chickens, the pigs, the once stubborn Swedish cow and the little field mouse and his family all lived happily ever after.

The Mean Old Man and the Single Chair

Introduction

The following story was inspired by a true story about a mean old man and his single chair. My friend Don Johnson told me this story and I have put more details into it. Nevertheless, I must thank Don for the basic outline and for the great way he told the story which as I said inspired me to write this tale. I hope you will enjoy it.

The Mean Old Man and the Single Chair

When I was a young boy my parents, two sisters and I lived in a mobile home or trailer as some would call them. Though, we never trailer-ed it anyplace. Villagers said we lived in a trailer park and kids at school would laugh and joke about us being "trailer trash." I got in many fights with other kids over these insults.

Every day, my sisters and I would walk to the pickup site for the school bus. Back in those days, kids could still go to school without a chaperone. We even went out Halloween trick or treating by ourselves and kept any food or candy that we collected. The one house we did not go to for tricks or treats belonged to a mean old man. My parents and the older kids in the trailer park warned us to stay away from his house. They all said that he was mean and hated everyone.

Each day after coming back from school, (School let out at about 3:15 PM) the school bus would drop us off. My sisters and I along with a few of my friends would walk home. We would go by the old man's house. He would inevitably be sitting on a makeshift porch in front of his trailer in an old rocking chair. We would stroll by his home and occasionally wave but he would never wave back. As we went by, he would fix a relentlessly hostile gaze on us which could put fear in anyone's heart. We imagined he was mad at the world and that certainly included us. Inevitably, we picked up our pace and tried to hurry by his place as fast as we could.

A few years passed and the mean old man simply seemed to grow meaner. One day after the bus dropped us off, a few of my friends and I were walking home. As we were passing the old man's home, he was sitting in his usual place and just staring at us. My friends started laughing at and taunting him with various insults.

"Hey grandpa, what's it like being so mean?"

"Hey old man, can you help us find our cat?"

I told them to stop it as he had never bothered anyone. They turned their taunts on me.

"Tim, if you like him so much, why don't you go talk to him. We dare you to go talk to him!"

They cried out at me: "Chicken! Chicken! Chicken!"

I tried to ignore their jibes, but finally, I had had enough. "I am not afraid. I will go talk to him." I started to walk down the path to where the old man was sitting. My heart began beating faster and faster. I wondered what I was going to say. Nothing occurred to me. The old man was staring at me intently. I could hear my friends laughing and hooting behind me.

As I reached the old man, he looked terribly angry.

"Ok", he said, "What do you want."

I said the first thing that came into my mind: "Well, I was just wondering why you don't have another chair so someone can sit and talk with you?"

"None of your business", he answered, "Now why don't you just run off and go back with your friends."

I could not think of another thing to say.

As I turned to leave, I said "Goodbye, have a nice day."

The old man mumbled something which I thought might be "same to you" but I could not be sure.

Saturday and Sunday passed quickly and Monday we were back in school. After school adjourned, I decided that I did not want to be go home with my usual friends, so I took the "late" bus from school. I got off at the bus stop and started home. As I passed the mean old man's house, he was sitting in his chair. Much to my surprise, he had a single chair sitting right next to him. Somewhat emboldened by this turn of events, I walked up the path to his house and stood in front of him again.

He looked at me and asked me "What do you want."

I replied, "Well, I notice that you have a single chair free, would you mind if I sat and talked to you for a while."

"OK" was all he said.

I sat down and started to tell him about all the things that I was doing in school. I told him about my classes, my teachers, and my friends. I talked about my parents, my sisters, and my grandparents. He listened intently to all I said and never interrupted or asked any questions. Realizing that it was getting late and that my parents would be worried, I said that I was going to go home but I would see him again tomorrow.

He simply nodded and mumbled, "Goodbye."

My trips and visits to the mean old man's house continued for many days. The days stretched into weeks. Over time, we started to talk more about his life. I found out that his name was Bill and that he had been married but his wife had died about ten years earlier. He had not had any children. Bill was a veteran and we talked about his wartime service and experiences. Bill was always more interested in what I was doing and asked me many questions about my school and life. Bill said that he did not have any friends and no surviving relatives.

I asked Bill if he did not have any friends in our local church, but he said that his wife had been the church goer. He had occasionally gone to church with her, but after she died, his stopped going. Bill confided in me that he had never been a social person and had always found it difficult to make friends. Most of the friends were his wife's friends and after she died, they stopped coming to visit. He was all alone now.

Weeks turned into months and it became my habit to routinely stop by Bill's house on my way home from school. We talked and I told him about my day, and he listened and asked questions which made me think a great deal about my choices and decisions in life. I could share things with Bill that I did not share with anyone else.

Then one day when I was coming home and passing Bill's house, I saw that someone else was sitting in the single chair. Not wanting to interrupt, I waved and walked on by. The next day we resumed our discussions as usual but the following day, the chair was again occupied. Over time, the single chair was alternately occupied by me and many other people.

I found out that Bill had started to go to church again and he had met people from all walks of life. Some were retired and some were not. The people who met Bill found him to be a remarkably interesting person. They would stop by and sit in the single chair next to Bill and talk about all their chosen topics.

High school came and went. Bill and I had many talks but just as often, he had someone else sitting in the chair when I came by. I went off to college and saw Bill much less except when I came home to visit my parents. Bill and I discussed writing to each other but we both agreed that we were not writers. I finished college and found a job in another city. My times with Bill had dwindled to a mere pittance of what they once had been.

A few more years passed by.

A message came from my parents notifying me that Bill had died. I came home to go to his funeral. It was well attended with nearly a hundred people to honor him. Many nice things were said about Bill. Everyone talked about what a good listener he was and how he always cared more about what others were doing or thinking. He was one of the least egocentric people you could have met.

About two weeks after the funeral, a letter arrived in my mail. It was from my hometown, but I did not recognize the address. I opened it up and inside were two pieces of stationary. First, I opened the one with the typing on it.

"We were going through some of Bill's possessions and we found this note on his bedside. We thought he meant to give it to you but never got around to mailing it."

I opened the second piece of stationary. It was in rough scrawl which I recognized as Bill's handwriting. I carefully read each word.

Dear Tim,
You are the best friend I ever had.
Thanks,
Bill

I still keep this note. It is perhaps the nicest compliment I have ever received. Whenever, I miss Bill, I pull this note out to remember him and the many talks we had. Bill is in his rocking chair and I am in the single chair beside him.

The Story of the Lost Frederic Treasure

Introduction

You are going to find the following story as unbelievable as I would have, had it not happened to me. In addition, for the skeptics out there, I am posting pictures of the actual treasure map that I recently found. No, I have not found the lost Frederic treasure yet, but given time, I think I will. Well, let's back up a minute so I can tell you the whole story.

About two weeks ago, I finally got the car that we left in the garage (a 1998 Saturn Coupe) running and out of the garage. The battery had died after having been left to sit in an unheated garage through one of the coldest winters in history up here. Since this is our run-about car, I wanted to put the 2009 Honda Civic in the garage. It is newer and more dependable. Karen generally uses it when we are up here in Frederic. By the way, Frederic is a town of about 1200 people in the Northwest area of Wisconsin, located in Polk County.

Karen's great grandparents (the Blomgrens) were early pioneers and residents in this area. They founded a mercantile store and a realty agency back in the early part of the twentieth century. There is a Blomgren road nearby. There are many Blomgrens interred in the local cemetery and even some Blomgren memorabilia in the Frederic History Center. We have a 1923 Frederic phone book with names of Blomgren family members who lived here as well as an old 1909 ceramic plate from the Blomgren Mercantile store.

Perhaps the most unique thing we actually own is an old wooden desk that was built in 1900 for William Starr (The original founder of Frederic. The town was named after his son) and at some time was acquired by Karen's grandfather. Well, Karen's father inherited the desk from his father and Karen eventually inherited the desk from her father. The desk came from Frederic and is now back in Frederic where it started out its life. I guess this old desk is determined to become a part of Frederic history.

After getting the Saturn out of the garage, I wanted to put the Civic in and put a remote in the car for the garage door. I had placed the remote in the house before we left to go to Arizona last October. After six months, I had forgotten where I had so carefully strategically placed it. Thus, began a search of the house which eventually led me to searching the old desk. That old desk has more drawers than I can count and was the last place to look.

A few years ago, we actually found an old 1910 deed to the Blomgren Cemetery Plot in one of the drawers. After contacting the Maple Grove Cemetery Association, we found that we were proud owners of a 1 and ½ cemetery plot that was still legal and valid after more than 100 years. Karen plans to take the full plot and I will take the ½ plot. I figure an urn with my ashes would fit nicely there. Even so, I must return to the story. Sorry for my digressions. It is just that I want you to fully understand the import of what I am about to tell you. This could forever change the history of this town and perhaps put Frederic on the map where it deserves to be. It is such a unique and interesting town. But that is a story for another day. I suppose you are getting anxious to know about the lost Frederic treasure.

Well, I finally found the garage door opener. What I found while looking for the opener is actually the beginning of this story. I found a secret compartment hidden behind one of the old pull-out drawers. I was rather amazed because we had been through this desk many times. In the compartment, I found a 1915 edition of a book titled: <u>New Standard American Business Guide</u>, copyright 1904 by Gordon G. Sapp. Since I love books, my first thought was to look through it to see what it was about. I quickly read the "Alphabetical Table of Contents" and was amazed at the wide range of subjects it included.

Starting from "Affidavits," it listed such topics as: banking, bills of exchange, farms and farming, mortgages, naturalization, and last, working on Sundays and legal holidays. Dare I say, I was amazed at the breadth and depth of the subject matter included in this book? If you could read this entire book, it would be like getting a BA degree in Business; albeit a BA in 1915, which today might make you somewhat obsolete. I put the book alongside of my other books (in my books to read pile), to either read or review later in the week.

The following day as I was leafing through the Sapp book, I found an old piece of faded typed parchment with the heading: **The Story of the Lost Frederic Treasure**. At first, I thought it might be a joke, yet after reading the manuscript; I began to wonder if it was sincere. I am a born skeptic and so I did some research into the history of Frederic to see whether or not there could be any validity to the entire story.

Lo and behold, the more I read about Frederic, the more I became convinced that this was truly a legitimate story. The history, dates, names, and places all matched up. I Googled about seventy-five different sources and the history was quite accurate. I gradually came to believe the story. The main theme was that about 150 years ago, William Starr had buried some type of treasure near Frederic in an old box. Whether it was gold, silver or someone's peculiar idea of a treasure could not be known until the treasure box was found. Putting the old book away, I went back to my other work.

Two more weeks went by before I picked up the old book again. I had totally forgotten the treasure and its story of mayhem and carnage. Everyone knows there is a treasure in the Superstition Mountains in Phoenix, but you won't find me looking for the supposed "Lost Dutchman Mine." I have better things to do then go up and down those mountains looking for buried gold. Now, if I had a map, it might be a different story. With this last thought in my mind, you will never believe what happened next.

As I continued scanning the old book, out fell another old piece of parchment with some archaic writing by pen and hand. It looked like some kind of a map. On it was written, "**Not ten leagues from the lake with the raccoons, the treasure box is buried.**" Now Frederic has a lake called Coon Lake and ten or less leagues would place the treasure box somewhere near Clam Falls, Wisconsin. I do not know how this map was created or who created it. This "treasure map" might have been drawn from a previous document by either Frederic Starr, son of William Starr or Karen's great grandfather or grandfather. Both who lived in Frederic and would have had some knowledge of the local area and traditions. Karen's great grandfather Gustav Blomgren came over from Sweden in 1870 when he was in his early twenties and settled just north of Frederic. Gustav died in the mid 1920's. Karen's grandfather Magnus Theodore Blomgren was the son of Gustav. Magnus was born in Frederic in 1884 and died in Frederic in 1976,

There is no doubt that the "treasure map" is more recent than the typed manuscript that I found since it includes both some old and more recent place names. The map is not as detailed as I would have liked. I have uploaded the map on my blog site at www.agingcapriciously.com/ Just go to the site and type in "The Lost Frederic Treasure." There is a good photo of the old desk and the map. I am not even going to sell the map. It is yours to use for free.

My two reasons for posting the map: Number one: Following the old map, I have had no luck. I have spent hours out digging and hunting but so far, my efforts have been fruitless. Since my days on this earth are more and more numbered, I would love to see the old treasure found even if it is not by me. Second reason: To assure you that there is truth to this story. All you have to do is come up to Frederic some Saturday with a pick and shovel and you may be the next millionaire. Perhaps more research might help pin down precisely where the treasure is located. There are many old records in the Frederic History Museum, the Frederic Library, and the Frederic Newspaper Office. Someone with more determination than I have had could likely find some clues to help locate the treasure.

I wish anyone with the patience and curiosity to seek the old Frederic treasure, the best of luck. One warning to any potential treasure hunters, watch out for bears, wolves, ticks, and deer flies. They are all murder up here in the summer. Following is a copy of the first manuscript that I found written by John Anderson.

The Story of the Lost Frederic Treasure

I worked for Mr. Starr for nearly 25 years until he died in 1921. Legend has it that a fortune in gems and gold was buried by William J. Starr in a strong box not far from Frederic. He did this to hide it from the Ojibwa Indians during the great Sioux Uprising of 1867.

William J. Starr, one of the founders of Frederic, had developed a home site here as early as 1865. Being a prospector at heart, he had moved to the area in search of precious minerals. He soon met a local Native woman whom he hired as a guide to the area. Eventually, they were betrothed and as luck would have it, she was the only daughter of the local Lakota Chief Bear Eyes. Chief Bear Eyes did not get along with the numerous Ojibwa tribes in the area and was something of an outcast. His clan had lived in the area for many generations and he was determined to stay where his ancestors had hunted and fished. Most of the Lakota had moved to Minnesota across the river from Wisconsin.

When the Lakota tribes to the south rebelled against the white settlers, Chief Bear Eyes decided to remain at peace with the white settlers this side of the St. Croix River. This decision did not set well with the local Ojibwa tribes as they had taken sides with the settlers and wanted to use the uprising as means of punishing the remaining Lakota in the area and sending them across the river to Minnesota.

One night in the late summer, Chief Bear Eyes learned of an impending attack on his clan by the Ojibwa tribes. He sent his daughter, Princess Nomokagen, who still lived with him together with a strong box to stay with William J. Starr until the battle was over. Starr and Princess Nomokagen decided it would be best to hide the strongbox. Local townsfolk claim they saw them put a large box that was about 3 feet by 3 feet on the back of a mule and head out in the woods somewhere to the east of where Frederic was eventually built. Apparently, after burying the box, William and the Princess made a small treasure map to guide them back to the strongbox. The original map was secreted at the home of Starr.

Unfortunately, Chief Bear Eyes and his entire clan were killed in the battle and the strong box was forgotten in the commotion that followed the battle and uprising. Princess Nomokagen was so distraught by the death of her family that she committed suicide by drowning in the Yellow River.

William Starr was saddened by the death of his betrothed but soon turned to more immediate interests. He had given up his quest for precious minerals when he realized that the abundance of large pine trees would be worth their weight in gold. He started one of the first logging camps in the area and soon became a millionaire lumber baron. He was president of the Davis and Starr Lumber Company and the Wisconsin Refrigerator Company, secretary of the Eau Claire Book and Stationery Company, owner and operator of an orchard and stock farm in Wisconsin and four farms and a large country estate where the family resided near Easton, Maryland. He hired me in 1901 as his bookkeeper and personal assistant.

Starr had large interests in the Steven and Jarvis Lumber Company of Eau Claire, Wisconsin, and the Florence-Louisiana Company of Vermillion Parish, Louisiana, and owned extensive timber lands in Wisconsin and California as well as the Parkdale Apartment Building in Chicago. He was a man of considerable standing in Frederic, the leading benefactor of the West Sweden Lutheran Church,

President of the first Frederic Public Library Board, and a member of numerous area clubs. He also seems to have had a wide acquaintance in both the political and financial arena. The town of Frederic, Wisconsin near to his first lumber camp was named after his youngest son. William J. Starr died in 1921. Starr had apparently forgotten all about the strong box that he had buried.

The story as told to me by his son was that on his death bed, Starr suddenly remembered the strong box that he had buried fifty-five years earlier. With his last dying breath, he tried to tell his son and heirs about the treasure and where the map was hidden. But, he was very weak and all they could barely hear him say: "map in house to gold, silver, buried nearby Frederic in woods."

I "John Anderson" bookkeeper and personal assistant to William J. Starr hereby testify that the above story and details are to the best of my knowledge true and accurate. _______________________________________

John Anderson died in 1959. My numerous attempts to find the treasure have all proven futile. Most of the people familiar with the story are now deceased. Some believe it was all a hoax and that no gold or treasure ever existed. Years later in 1971 one of Starr's great-grandchildren found a Lakota cooking pot made of solid gold in the old attic of Starr's house in Maryland. The single pot weighted six pounds and was conservatively valued at $3,900 dollars. This find gave some credibility to the old tale of Frederic's lost treasure.

With the finding of the treasure map that I have uploaded, rough as it may be, I invite you to find the **Lost Frederic Treasure**. My efforts towards this task suggests that the treasure box is buried somewhere under what is now a lake or swamp in the area. The geography and topography are quite different now than it was years ago. Eventually, someone will succeed and find the treasure box. I hope it will be you.

Good Luck and Happy Hunting!

Ed, the Soldier

Introduction

I include in this book several stories that I patterned somewhat after the book **Spoon River Anthology** by Edward Lee Masters. My stories are about suffering and abused people that speak for themselves from the dead. They write their own biographies or autobiographies. I am not sure which term is correct since my authors are all deceased. In these stories, they question the reasons for living and the reasons for dying. They want you to know what their living and dying was for. Ed the Soldier will tell you the story of his life and death. It is typical of the stories that I have heard from many veterans who served in far and away places where they did not know what they were fighting for or even who they are fighting.

Ed, the Soldier

I was brave and loyal. I gave my all for the corps. I was taught to respect and obey authority. Right or wrong, it was my job to follow orders. I never questioned my assignments. I never questioned my Sergeant or my Captain. As was said in the famous poem, "mine was to do or die and not to question why." I am looking now at my body and those of my nine squad members. We had one medic, three guys with M-16's, one guy with an MGL-140, one guy with a Barrett .338 Lapua Magnum, one guy with an MPIM/SRAW rocket, one radio guy or in this case a radio gal, Sarge our Squad Leader and of course me carrying a good old US issue M-16 along with a bunch of grenades.

It was all over so quickly. It looks like my arms and chest have been shot full of holes. However, I think it was the two bullets that caught me in my brain which finished me off. My head looks like it was stuck in a meat grinder. Most of my squad does not look much better. There are a few guys minus heads, some missing legs and others missing body parts. A good jigsaw puzzler could not put us all back together again. I can't believe the number of bullets that hit us. One minute we were joking around and the next minute it sounded like a Fourth of July celebration. The difference being that we were the targets, and the bullets and the rockets were lighting us up instead of the sky. What happened to our vaunted Intel?

I enlisted right out of high school. I did not want to go to college, and I could not think of anything else to do. I went down to my Army recruiting office and was scheduled immediately with an appointment. I did not have to wait long. About thirty minutes later, a well-dressed very sharp looking soldier came out of an office to greet me.

"Son," he began, "You have come to the right place. We will fix you up so that you can serve your country and really make a difference in the world. Do you want your parents and friends to look up to you? Do you want to be get laid more than you could ever dream possible? Do you want to be a real hero and not some phony cardboard actor hero, then just sign right here?" I signed up immediately.

"My boy, you have just saved the free world. Welcome to the US Army."

After basic training, they announced that I had been selected for a tour in Iraq. They said it would be easy duty. It would just be some mopping up operations and nothing really tough. The really tough stuff had been done months before. And besides that, the "ragheads" could not shoot straight, so we had nothing to worry about. Each day we went out on patrol to a different village or to a specific part of the same village. The "ragheads" all looked alike. Some of the local men were friendly with our soldiers, but most just ignored us. Kids would come over and ask us for candy or cigarettes when they would see us walking. The women really kept to themselves. You hardly ever saw any on the street and if you did, they were always covered from head to toe. We were taught to trust no one but after a while you got to know certain kids and we would give them candy or sometimes some money.

We were not allowed to have any alcohol as it is illegal in Muslim countries. There wasn't much to do all day long except when we were on patrol. Most of the fun we had was out in the villages. We loved to play pranks on each other. On one patrol, one of the guys had hidden behind a wall and as we started to walk by, he threw a dummy grenade at us. We scattered like rabbits and waited for it to go off. After a few seconds, we could hear laughter coming from behind the wall. We soon realized that it was one of our guys. He was laughing so hard; it gave him cramps. It took us weeks, but we figured out how to get even with him. I guess we were always really wound up when out on patrol, so it was not hard to find something to break up the tension. Often it would involve shooting at anything that seemed sinister or menacing.

The day we got hit was like any other day, nothing unusual about it. It was bright, sunny, and warm. We had an assignment to check out a village that had been quiet for some time. We were on foot patrol. Ten of us were joking and clowning around. Some kids had just run by and yelled, "Go home Americans!" We threw some candy at them and laughed as they scrambled to pick it up. As we turned the corner of a street, we saw some quick movement in a doorway and some guys running across the roof tops. We raised our rifles to fire, but it was too late. The grenades and RPGs burst all around us and then the AK 47 fire started. We never had a chance. There must have been about fifty of them. We never thought that there were that many bad guys left. One by one we went down. I never even got off a round.

I can see them now. They are picking over our bodies. They are taking cash, weapons, armor, and anything else of value. The little kids we knew are there too. They are kicking us in the heads or what is left of our heads. I even saw one kid who I thought was my friend (I gave him many Snicker bars) come running up and kick me in my head. He then took out his wiener and pissed on me. It seemed like a holiday for them. They are all so happy. It was just a big celebration. They are laughing and patting each other on the back. I can hear one guy in English saying: "I guess these fucking Americans will go home now." Another one replied: "Yeah, home or Jahannam."

I know I was supposed to be a hero. I thought I was making the world safe for democracy. Where did it all go wrong? Looking down at our bodies now, it does not seem like we really accomplished much. It looks like they would have been happier if we had never come. I guess I might be a hero when my body comes back to Ohio. I never got laid either.

I can't hang around here much longer. I can't bear the sadness. It is time to leave. I was brought up to be a good Christian. I am sure that there must be a reason for all this. My pastor said, "God's ways are unknowable." I am going to

go find God. I am sure he can tell me what this was all for.

The Fox and the Rabbit

Introduction

Growing up I always loved the Uncle Remus stories and the Aesop fables. The following story melds elements of both authors. If you have never read tales from either source, you are missing one of the great treasure troves of morals ever written. Here is my contribution to the genre of fables with a moral.

The Fox and the Rabbit

It was shortly after the race between Mr. Rabbit and Mr. Tortoise. Everyone was still talking about how Mr. Tortoise had beaten Mr. Rabbit. The unthinkable had happened. How could the slowest moving creature in the forest beat one of the speediest forest creatures? Of course, the entire episode was an example of how pride and hubris could be the downfall of anyone. Mr. Rabbit was so certain that he could beat the tortoise that he played the fool and lost the race. However, Mr. Rabbit assured everyone that he was too smart to ever let this happen again.

The wise old fox was getting long in tooth and short in speed. Years ago, he would have had a chance to catch a rabbit for dinner, but those times were mostly history now. Instead, Mr. Fox knew that he must rely on stealth and not speed. Only by using his wit and cunning could he avoid starvation in old age.

Now Mr. Fox had observed the race between the rabbit and the tortoise. He had observed the strutting and pompousness of Mr. Rabbit. He has also heard Mr. Rabbit assure everyone that such a situation would never happen again. Mr. Fox had another idea though and he thought, "This might just be the opportunity that I am waiting for. I think that leopards rarely change their spots, and I will test my theory on Mr. Rabbit."

A few weeks went by and one day Mr. Rabbit and Mr. Fox were crossing intersecting trails when Mr. Fox spied Mr. Rabbit and decided to put his plan into action. He yelled to Mr. Rabbit, "Can you wait just a minute; I have a challenge for you?" Mr. Rabbit, always extremely competitive and certain that Mr. Fox was nowhere close enough to grab him, answered back, "What kind of a challenge Mr. Fox?"

"I want to challenge you to a race just like the one you had with Mr. Tortoise," replied Mr. Fox. Now Mr. Rabbit knew that Mr. Fox was very cunning, but he also knew that Mr. Fox had grown old and slow. He decided to play out the game because he was curious to see what Mr. Fox was up to. "What's in it for me if I beat you?" asked Mr. Rabbit, confident that there was no way Mr. Fox could beat him. "Well, said Mr. Fox, if you win, I will bring you a bushel full of carrots to eat. If I win, you will bring me a bushel full of wheat." Mr. Fox did not really care for wheat, but he needed to show that he thought he just might win.

Mr. Rabbit, still suspicious of a trick answered, "Well, I am agreeable to the race but on one condition. If I win, you must deliver the carrots to me at a place and time that I will specify." Surely, he thought, there will be no chance for Mr. Fox to grab me if I have him deliver the carrots to my warren. Mr. Fox was agreeable to the terms for truth be told, the situation was working out just as he had hoped it would.

Mr. Rabbit assumed that Mr. Fox would try to somehow grab him during the race, and he was not going to let this happen. No sleeping or napping during this race. He would move so fast that he would blow the pants off Mr. Fox. The word went out through the forest that Mr. Rabbit was going to be in another race. His opponent this time would be Mr. Fox. The entire forest was abuzz with anticipation. All knew that for many years, Mr. Fox had tried to catch Mr. Rabbit but with no results. What was he up to, was the thought on everyone's mind,

The day of the race came. Mr. Rabbit and Mr. Fox took their respective places. Mr. Rabbit made sure he was nowhere close to Mr. Fox at the starting line. Hundreds of forest creatures had arrived to watch the big race. Mr. Owl blew the starting whistle and off they went. Over hill, over dale, through the thickest parts of the forest ran Mr. Fox and Mr. Rabbit. However, Mr. Fox was clearly outmatched. Mr. Rabbit was hundreds of yards ahead. He had such a lead that he could not even see Mr. Fox. He thought to himself, "Mr. Fox thinks I am going to take a nap and catch me, but he is too stupid for me. I will keep going until I reach the finish line." Minutes later, Mr. Rabbit crossed the finish line and Mr. Fox was nowhere in sight. Mr. Rabbit jumped up and down and shouted things like, "Stupid old fox, thought he could catch me." "Mr. Fox has gotten senile in his old age if he thinks that he can outsmart me."

Mr. Fox finally crossed the finish line many minutes later than Mr. Rabbit. Mr. Rabbit had grown tired of waiting and he left a note for Mr. Fox with Mr. Owl. "Please give this note to Mr. Fox from me" he asked, "It has directions for when and where he should bring the carrots that he owes me." Mr. Fox took the note and went home.

A week or so passed and Mr. Fox had collected all the carrots that would fit into a bushel basket. He also collected a few more that he was going to put into a gunny sack. He put a note on the bushel basket that he had picked more carrots than required by the bet, but he was going to donate them to Mr. Rabbit anyway. Furthermore, he left the sack to make it easier for Mr. Rabbit to get his carrots home. All these items were left at the requested time and place on the path to the rabbit's home.

Mr. Rabbit walked by, saw his prize and thought, "My, my! I guess Mr. Fox knows who the better runner is now. That stupid fox will think twice before he challenges me again." Mr. Rabbit grabbed a carrot and promptly ate it. After eating a few more carrots, he decided it was time to get them back home. It would not do to be out after dark.

Mr. Rabbit managed to carry the basket home and then came back for the sack. Letting his guard down, Mr. Rabbit did not notice that Mr. Fox had snuck back to the site where the sack was and climbed inside it. Mr. Rabbit grabbed the sack and tried to throw it over his shoulder, but it was too heavy. "What is in this sack?" thought Mr. Rabbit. He opened it to peer inside and before you could say "Jack Rabbit," Mr. Fox had Mr. Rabbit in his jaws. Sad to say, that was the end of Mr. Rabbit.

Now, any good story must have a moral and that goes double for stories with an unhappy ending. I have tried to find a fitting moral to this tale. There are perhaps several morals that might fit.

- Beware of Greeks bearing gifts.

- Pride goes before a fall.

- The leopard does not change its spots.

- Always keep your enemies in sight.

- Long-term thinking will always win out over short-term thinking.

Mr. Fox was not sure which of these morals he had followed. He only knew that rabbit was a mighty tasty morsel when served cold.

It's Coming Quick. It's Coming Quick. The End is Coming Quick

Introduction

I always loved the Winnie-the-Pooh Bear stories by A. A. Milne. The stories are delightful, imaginative, and touching. I wonder if we all love these stories so much because we see some of ourselves in the Pooh Bear. Someone who wants to do the right thing is often confused by life and so settles for the simple luxuries and pleasures he can find. Here is my contribution to the genre. I hope you enjoy it.

It's Coming Quick. It's Coming Quick, the End is Coming Quick

Winnie-the-Pooh was walking home one day when he passed a young man standing on a park bench. The young man was shouting "Quick, it's coming quick. It's coming quick. The end is coming quick."

This greatly distressed the Pooh Bear who ran home as fast as his bear legs could carry him. After arriving home, he made a big honey and jelly sandwich on toast. He had been saving this honey for a special occasion but since the end was coming quick, he decided he had better eat it as soon as he was able to. After this, Pooh straightened up his abode and waited. He might as well wait for the end to happen while he was home and warm and comfortable and feeling very nourished after his honey and jelly on toast sandwich.

But you know Pooh Bears; they are not very patient. Soon Winnie-the-Pooh became restless and started wondering when the end was coming. He began pacing back and forth and forth and back - and the end still did not come. Finally, losing patience, Pooh decided to visit his good friend Eeyore to see if he had any news on the end. After a short trek over to where Eeyore lived in his house made of sticks, the two good friends met and embraced each other. Quickly, Eeyore started worrying and wondering what was going to happen. If Pooh Bear came to see him, something must be wrong. Eeyore finally blurted out, "Pooh, what is up? What is happening? why are you here?" Pooh knew that Eeyore was easily unsettled but he felt that this situation warranted unsettling poor Eeyore. Pooh said. "Eeyore, the end is coming quick." "Oh my, oh my," lamented Eeyore, "that is a problem. What do you think we should do?" Pooh replied well "Do you have any honey or jelly? We could make some honey and jelly sandwiches and wait for the end." Eeyore was not fond of honey and jelly sandwiches, but he had some good hay and aged straw that he had been saving. He then invited Pooh to share it with him. This was not exactly what Pooh had in mind, but he watched and paced back and forth and forth and back, while Eeyore ate his aged straw.

Finally, after a long time had passed (It was actually a short time, but it seemed long to Pooh and Eeyore), they both became restless again. When was the end going to come? Pooh suggested that they both go to visit Tigger since he is always optimistic and might have a different view on things. Hurrying over to Tigger's house, they find him in the front yard playing with a balloon while bouncing up and down on a trampoline. "Hi!" greets Tigger, "Do you guys want to bounce on my trampoline." "No, no" says Eeyore, "this is serious. The end of coming quick, we must be ready." "Fine with me" says Tigger, "but can't we just bounce and play until the end comes?" "Well," says Pooh, "that would be fine, but I am getting hungry. Do you happen to have any honey or jelly that I could make a sandwich with?" "Sorry Pooh, but my cupboard is bare, I have been too busy bouncing to worry about eating." So the three friends decided to just wait together for the end. Tigger kept bouncing and bouncing. Pooh kept feeling hungry and Eeyore kept fretting since he was becoming less and less certain that anything was really going to happen.

Eventually after a long bout of bouncing, Tigger became tired. "I am going to take a nap." If the end is coming, I would just as soon be rested when it does." Eeyore more and more doubting that the end was really coming or at least that it would be quick decided to go home. "Bye, Pooh. See you later" said Eeyore; "that is if there really is a later." Pooh was left all alone. Tired, hungry, and confused, he was not sure what to do. Then, in a flash, it came to him. "I will go to see Owl. He is the wisest animal in the forest. He will know what to do." So Pooh went off to see Owl.

Owl saw Pooh coming from a long way off. Owl was perched up in his nest. "Welcome" said Owl. "What brings you to the forest today? Are you here to discuss the ethics of Aristotle or maybe you have come to hear about my life when I was a young owl about your age? Did I ever tell you about the time that I met…"? "Ahem, ahem", interrupts Pooh. This is an emergency! The end is coming quick. We must be ready. I tried to warn Eeyore and Tigger, but Tigger decided to take a nap and Eeyore went home. What are we to do?" "My, my," said Owl. "You say the end is coming quick. Pray tell me what end is coming: the end of the ball game, the end of the warm weather, the end of the hunting season?" All of these questions simply confused Pooh. He had no idea what end was coming. He just assumed it meant the end of the world. Why did Owl always have to make things so complicated? "Well," said Pooh, "I am not really sure. I saw this young boy (who looked a lot like Christopher Robin) standing on a park bench shouting that the end was coming quick. I am not really sure what end he meant now that you have confused me so. I just came to ask you for advice on what to do. I am all out of honey and jelly and the end is coming quick.”

Owl thought about the situation and came up with the following poem that he had heard many years before: “A Song on the End of the World” by Czeslaw Milosz, 1944.

On the day the world ends
A bee circles a clover,
A fisherman mends a glimmering net.
Happy porpoises jump in the sea,
By the rainspout young sparrows are playing
And the snake is gold-skinned as it should always be.

On the day the world ends
Women walk through the fields under their umbrellas,
A drunkard grows sleepy at the edge of a lawn,
Vegetable peddlers shout in the street
And a yellow-sailed boat comes nearer the island,
The voice of a violin lasts in the air
And leads into a starry night.

And those who expected lightning and thunder
Are disappointed.
And those who expected signs and archangels’ trumps
Do not believe it is happening now.
As long as the sun and the moon are above,
As long as the bumblebee visits a rose,
As long as rosy infants are born
No one believes it is happening now.

Only a white-haired old man, who would be a prophet

Yet is not a prophet, for he's much too busy,
Repeats while he binds his tomatoes:
There will be no other end of the world,
There will be no other end of the world.

Pooh honestly did not know what this poem meant or why Owl was telling it to him. "Owl!" exclaimed Pooh. "You are hurting my brain. I am even more confused now then I was before. Couldn't we keep this simple?" "Of course," said Owl, "animals and people always want things simple. But maybe, this is not so simple as you would think. Perhaps we should discuss this further." "No, let's not" replied Pooh. "I am too hungry now to worry about the end. All I know is my stomach is growling and I need to find some honey quick to cure the rumbly in my tummy. In fact, maybe that is what the boy was trying to tell me. I must find honey very quick or the end will be near for me."

Pooh thanked Owl for his time and obtuse advice. He then ran off to find some honey. By the time, Pooh returned home, he had found a big stash of honey and had totally forgotten that the end was near. Pooh made a great big honey sandwich and settled in with a large mug of hot chocolate. As long as he had good friends, honey, and a comfortable home, that darn end (whatever it was) could come whenever it wanted to.

The Man Who Was Smarter Than God

Introduction

A number of years ago, I chanced upon the quote, "What Wisdom can you find that is greater than Kindness?" (Jean Jacques Rousseau). Growing up with a father who seemed to value intelligence above all else, this quote was a profound experience for me. Seldom have I ever encountered a comment that has made me think more about my own life and values. I am not the man in this story, but I sympathize with Michael in many ways. I once believed that I could solve all of the problems in the world, if only I were smart enough. I had little use for stupidity and the people who I thought did not measure up to my standards.

The Man Who Was Smarter than God

Once upon a time there was a man who was smarter than God. At least that is what his people said behind his back. Michael was indeed one of the smartest men you could ever meet. Now some might call this a blessing, while others might call it a curse. His mother was fond of saying that "Ignorance is bliss." His father believed (though he did not practice it himself) that intellect and knowledge were everything. A man who was smart enough could rule the world. His father continually berated Michael to think and to use his intellect. He demanded that Michael read only non-fiction. In an argument, Michael should stick to the facts. The only things that mattered in the world were facts. Emotions ruled stupid people and decisions based on emotions were decisions that were stupid.

Michael grew up with little respect or tolerance for anyone or anything that was not logical and rationale. When the first Star Trek series became popular, Michael was surprised at the admiration for Lt. Commander Spock. Many people saw Spock as the epitome of logic and rational thinking versus Kirk's impulsiveness and McCoy's rampant emotionalism. However, Michael saw Spock as divided between emotions and intellect. He could not accept that Spock was a role model for logical thinking. Nothing was as important to Michael as mind, intellect, and the ability to ignore and suppress emotions. This of course had its negative side as far as Michael's social aspirations were concerned.

Michael had no male friends and zero female friends. Men did not like Michael because they feared his put downs and lack of acceptance of their often biased and illogical thinking. Michael was intolerant of what he saw as inept thinking and had no qualms about correcting anyone. It was hard to deny that Michael was usually right, but this meant that being around him would make you feel inferior and stupid. No one wants to associate with anyone who makes them feel insignificant.

Michael was attracted to women, would have liked to date them, and have a social relationship with the opposite sex. However, most women saw him as wooden and unemotional of which Michael was rather proud. Moreover, compassion and love were traits that Michael saw as incompatible with a rational human being. These traits would lead to decisions based on emotions and not logic. Dates that Michael went on with the opposite sex usually lasted less than an hour. Phone calls for a second date by Michael would always go unanswered.

Somewhere along the line, some of Michael's friends (more like acquaintances really) tagged him with the moniker, "The man who was smarter than God." This was the source of endless jokes and laughter, all behind Michael's back. He grew more and more isolated from any human contact, particularly after his mother and father died. Michael never even bothered to attend their funerals. "They are dead," he reasoned. "So my going to their funeral is not going to bring them back."

As the years went by, Michael became lonelier and lonelier but also richer and richer. Michael was a genius with computers and finance. He invested his money earned from writing software programs into a stock portfolio which grew to nine figures. He never had to worry about working for a living or where his next meal would come from.

Michael loved to take walks to break up his work and enjoyed being outside. One day while taking a walk, he stopped at a bench in a park and sat down to take a short rest. A young man about 16 years of age walked up to the bench and sat down next to Michael. "Hi," the young man said, "my name is Joshua, and I am special." "That's nice," replied Michael, hoping to end the conversation quickly. "I am running away from home," came back a reply. "Oh," said Michael, not particularly caring why. "Nobody likes me," explained Joshua. "My sister makes fun of me and my mom and dad don't do anything about it." Somewhat curious, Michael asked "Where are you going to go?" "I always go to this bench until it's time to go home" answered Joshua. This did not make any sense to Michael, so he continued the conversation to find out more about this strange boy.

Joshua was fifteen years old and a developmentally disabled child. He had suffered a fall when he was young which left him with both severely diminished cognitive capacity and physical limitations. Now in high school he spent most of his time in special needs classes. From early on his family told him he was special. They were loving parents and did their best to help him cope with his limited capacities. They knew he would never be able to live on his own. His older sister, Inez, whom Joshua loved dearly, frequently became exasperated with him. She loved him as much as he loved her, but she did not quite have the patience of their mother and dad. Every day about this time, she would go out looking for Joshua. The typical pattern was that he would become angry with her and "run away from home" to this park bench. Inez would come and "find" him and take him home.

Their conversation finally ended when Inez showed up. Joshua introduced Michael as his new friend to Inez. She said hello to Michael and that she was happy that Joshua had a new friend. Joshua asked Michael if he could come to visit Michael after school sometime if he did not live too far away. Michael reluctantly gave his address to them thinking that he would never see Joshua again. In some respects he regretted this since he actually felt a stirring of compassion towards Joshua and he was moved by Joshua's openness and lack of pretentiousness. Goodbyes all around and each left to go home.

Two days later, much to Michael's surprise, who should knock at his door but Inez and Joshua. Inez said that she would drop Joshua off if it was okay with Michael and pick him up in an hour. Michael agreed and spent the next hour talking to Joshua about many different things. Joshua was surprisingly able to comprehend many things that Michael would bring up and they had some interesting if eclectic conversations.

Michael learned that Joshua loved science, animals, and nature. He also learned that Joshua's parents were not wealthy. Michael deduced that they did not have enough money to buy some of the things that Joshua wanted. They often struggled to buy some of the things he needed. The fall has resulted in brain damage to Joshua and some severe internal injuries which needed ongoing treatment. Joshua never complained though and saw most of these hardships as simple facts of his life.

The first day that Michael and Joshua spent together turned into weeks and the weeks turned into months. Each week Michael and Joshua would spend at least an hour together. Some days Michael would play video games with Joshua and on other days they would do "walk and talks." Inez would drop Joshua off and Michael would take Joshua home. Michael looked forward each week to seeing Joshua and spending time with him. Michael offered to buy Joshua some of the things that he wanted, but Joshua's parents were proud and explained that they would prefer that he did not buy things for him. Michael accepted their request but would take Joshua out for a hamburger or pizza whenever possible. His parents did not mind this as Joshua had a prodigious appetite.

A few years went by and Michael's life became less lonelier and much happier. Michael greeted people on the street and spent time talking to other people without correcting them or giving them advice. Every week Michael and Joshua would get together. Then one-week Joshua did not come by. Michael was disappointed but simply thought that some event had come up and Joshua had to attend it. The following week went by and again no Joshua. By now, Michael was very worried. He called Joshua's parents. Inez answered and explained that they were at the hospital with Joshua who was seriously ill. She was sorry she had not come by to tell him about it, but things had been rather chaotic. She said Joshua had asked about Michael and when would he come up to visit. Michael told her that he would go right now.

When Michael arrived at the hospital, he found Joshua in bed with several tubes sticking out of him and his worried parents at his bedside. Joshua looked up when Michael entered his room and his face turned into a big smile. "I knew you would come," he happily exclaimed with a soft voice. "I am dying," he whispered to Michael. "But don't worry about it. I will be OK."

Michael stayed until Joshua fell asleep and then went out of the room followed by Joshua's parents. "We are sorry we did not call you sooner," they apologized. "We always knew this time would come, but we thought he had a few more years." "Isn't there anything they can do?" asked Michael. "No," replied his father. "We wish there was, but they have done everything they could."

Michael went every day to visit Joshua in the hospital. Then one day Joshua was no longer in the room. The nurse explained that Joshua had died in his sleep the night before. Funeral arrangements were made by Joshua's parents. At the funeral, Michael gave his condolences to Inez and Joshua's parents. Michael was nearly as devastated as they were. Joshua had a simple funeral, but Michael had arranged for plenty of flowers to be there.

Michael went home and for the next week did nothing and said nothing. Then one day he thought, I am not going to forget Joshua. I am sitting on a pile of money that is not doing anything for anyone. I am going to start a home for "special" children like Joshua where they can come to play games, have meals, and interact with toys that their parents could not afford for them to have. My home will have first class aides that are well trained in caring for special needs children. We will have all the security needed to ensure that these children have a safe environment. This will be someplace that parents can drop their children off when they need a break or rest.

So Michael started this home. It had the capacity for 150 children. The home had numerous playrooms, security cameras in each room and a full kitchen staffed by cooks with degrees in dietary nutrition. The home was free to qualified children. Acceptance was based on need and not income. Parents would fill out an application and it was reviewed by a board of professionals who were versed in the needs of special education children.

Michael named the home: "The Joshua Home for Children." He came each day and spent at least four hours. During these visits, he would meet the parents of each child and spend time with all the children to find out how they were doing and what they liked and did not like about the home. Michael was constantly making improvements. When he was there, he was using his genius to earn more money that he would then plow back into the home. Michael was admired by parents and loved by the children for the care and compassion.

Twenty years went by and Michael died. Before he died, he had set up a foundation and trust to manage the home. Every penny in his will went back into

the home. Michael had specified that he did not want an elaborate funeral.
Despite his request, the number of people who called to inquire about his funeral
soon dictated that his wish would go unheeded. Several unnamed benefactors put
up money to have the funeral moved to a larger venue. Even with a bigger
church, there was standing room only. Estimates were that over a thousand
people attended Michael's funeral. Many people stood up to talk about his
generosity and his compassion for children. His benevolence had extended not
only to the home but often to medical expenses and medical care that parents in
the community could not afford.

And not a single person referred to him or even thought of him as: **"The man
who was smarter than God."**

Four Young Boys Growing Up in America

Introduction

One of the great principles that America was founded on is the concept of equality. **"We hold these truths to be self-evident, that all men in America are created equal."** Do we believe that all men in America are created equal? Reading between the lines of the daily newspaper, or watching the daily news on the TV, we see how false this idea turns out to be in practice. Women, Blacks, Latinas, Asians, LGBTQ people and even children are still fighting battles for equality in the US of A. This story deals with some of the inequality that exists in the real world in the USA.

Four Young Boys Growing Up in America

Once upon a time, there were four boys. Their names were Jack, Whitaker, Jamal, and Robert. They were born and growing up in the United States of America. The land of the free and the home of the brave. Each boy was now entering his twelfth year of life. Each boy lived within ten miles of the other boys.

Jack was a white boy. His mother was of Italian heritage and his father's descendants were from Ireland. Both of Jack's parents were Catholic. Jack's mother worked as a cook in a small bakery in the town where they lived. Their town was now a suburb, as the nearby city had grown large enough to encompass most of what had once been a small town. Jack's father was a computer systems analyst working in the nearby city. He had gone to a local community college where he finished a two-year program in Information Technology (IT).

Jack went to a public school close to his home. Most of his school population was white but there were a few black students at the school. Jack was a friendly kid who never started fights or picked on anyone. He was an average student and seldom got A's on any subjects. On the whole, Jack was just another average white boy in a school full of other average white boys. His parents were hopeful that he would go to college and find a career with good prospects. His parents had started a college fund for Jack and believed that with some scholarships and loans, Jack would be able to afford the local public college.

Jack was taught that he would be successful if he worked hard, was honest and obtained a good education. He was taught to respect all people and that he should never judge anyone by the color of their skin, but only by what was inside of them. Jack grew up with a modest number of toys and once in a while even had a few designer clothes to wear.

Whitaker was a white boy. His mother was Scottish, and his father was English. It was said that his parents could both trace their heritage to some of the original Mayflower colonists. His parents were Presbyterian. Whitaker's mother was a lawyer in a large law firm in the city. Whitaker's father was a wealthy investor and a business owner in the city. They lived in an exclusive gated community within the same small town as Jack and his parents, though their paths never crossed.

Whitaker went to a private school in a nearby suburb. Whitaker was a rather moody boy, but he excelled in sports and was on the A list for most of his subjects in school. His parents shopped at an expensive supermarket and at the high-end retail stores in the city. Both parents drove Porsches and belonged to an exclusive private country club. They believed that wealth had its privileges, and they had many influential friends. They had no doubt that when it came time for Whitaker to go to college (There was never any question of whether or not he would go) that they could get him into either Yale or Harvard.

Whitaker was taught that people got what they deserved in life. If you worked hard and smart, then you would get ahead. If you did get ahead, it was because you earned it and you should never be ashamed of taking the lead or getting more of the good life. He was taught that life was on the whole fair. People should not be judged by what color they were, but what they had achieved in life. It was up to each individual to forge their own destiny. He did not worry about clothes or toys, since he simply needed to ask for what he wanted, and he would get it.

Jamal was a black boy. His mother and father had both grown up in the same city where they now lived. Jamal's grandparents had grown up in the Deep South and it was said that his great grandparents had worked as slaves on some plantation in Georgia. Jamal's mother and father belonged to an African Episcopal Methodist Church in the city. Jamal's mother worked as a Licensed Practical Nurse (LPN) in the local hospital. Jamal's father was an electrician in the same hospital and a member of the International Brotherhood of Electrical Workers (IBEW).

Jamal went to a public school in the city which was forty percent black, ten percent Latino, five percent Asian and forty-five percent white. Jamal was well liked in school and looked forward to going to school each morning. Jamal had friends from many different backgrounds. He was an exceptional student. He loved math and science. He was ok in sports but would rather hang out with the nerds than with the jocks. Jamal dreamed of going to college and was hopeful that someday he would be able to get into college.

Jamal was taught to be courteous to all people. In the final result, it was what was in someone's heart and not what they wore or the color of their skin that mattered. He was also taught that life was not fair. His parents cautioned him to be careful around white people, especially white police officers. Jamal learned that black people were not always treated like white people, but that he should not let this discourage him. He could still make something of himself in the world, but it would take more effort on his part.

Robert was a white boy. Robert did not know much about his father. His father left when Robert was still a baby. Robert grew up with a stepfather who told him that his birth father was a loser and a boozer. His stepfather was a construction worker in the city who worked long hours and when he wasn't working, he mostly watched football and baseball games. Once in a while, he would take Robert to the shooting range with him. He told Robert that it was important to learn how to shoot, so that he could protect himself.

Robert's mother was a recovering alcoholic. She worked part-time as a nurse's aide in a local assisted living center. She thought that her genealogy was a mixture of French, German, Irish, and even some Native American, although she was not certain of the amounts. She loved her son very much but was usually working when he came home from school. She would have liked to help him more with his schoolwork, but her shift work made that difficult. Robert's parents were hard working individuals but neither of them had much education or a love for learning. They did belong to a local evangelical church where they took Robert every Sunday.

Robert went to a public school in the city. It was the same school that Jamal attended. Robert hung with mostly the white boys. He loved sports but did not have much use for any of the academic subjects. He was typically disruptive in his classes, usually because he was bored. He saw little relevance in the academic subjects that could apply to his life. Although he knew his mother wanted him to go to college, Robert thought that he would really like to be a pro football player. He hoped that he could get into college on a sports scholarship and play football. If not, he would go into the United States Army.

Robert was taught not to take any shit from anyone. He was taught that people will take advantage of you if you let them. He learned in Sunday church school that Christians had built America and that immigrants were people who wanted something for nothing. His parents taught him to be careful about what he said about other people because the government was obsessed with politically correctness. It was not OK to say the truth about women and minorities. Saying the truth could result in people looking down on you. Thus, it was best to keep your mouth shut unless you were with other God-fearing Christian white people.

Twenty years have gone by since we have left our four young men. They have now each reached their 32nd year of life. Not one of them will see their 33rd year of life.

Whitaker had achieved everything his parents had wanted him to. He had gone to college, taken over the family business, got married to a beautiful young debutante and now had two young children. The oldest, a girl, was nine years old and a boy seven years old. Whitaker loved his wife and children. Like his parents, Whitaker joined the prestigious country club and was head of the planning committee for events.

His investment business was going very well, and his many clients were always pleased with the way that that their accounts were growing. Whitaker seemed to have a magic touch. Everything that was bronze or copper, he could turn into silver or gold. His family life was also picture perfect. Two well-mannered children and a stay-at-home wife. She alternated time between home and volunteering on various local committees to help the less fortunate in the community.

It was a beautiful Saturday morning in May. Apple blossoms were blooming. Whitaker had breakfast with his family and kissed each of them goodbye as they left for their day's activities.   His wife was planning a dinner that evening with some friends and his kids had their usual Saturday morning league sports. Whitaker told this family that he was going to the country club. There was some business to attend to with the club planning committee and if he had enough time, he might get in a round of golf. He took his golf bag and left for the country club.

Whitaker arrived at the club around 9 AM. He greeted some friends upon arrival and then went up to an office that he kept in a private room at the club. He entered the office and locked the door. He walked over to his desk and sat down. From a locked drawer in his desk, he removed a Ruger 9 mm automatic pistol.

He looked at it for a minute as though undecided, but finally he flicked the safety off. Whitaker put the gun to his head and pulled the trigger. He died instantly. Club members hearing the loud report rushed up to the room. They had to batter the door down. When they entered, they found Whitaker slumped over his desk and quite dead.

Jamal was heading to the country club about the time that Whitaker decided to depart this life. Jamal had gone to college and obtained a law degree. He had married the woman of his dreams and had a set of five-year-old twin girls. Jamal was a brilliant orator and could remember facts and figures that would astonish his listeners. His law firm had prospered, and he had two partners with more clients than even they could handle.

Jamal had moved from the inner city to a well-manicured upscale home in the elite section of town. He had a swimming pool, jacuzzi, a three-car garage and two large stone fireplaces in his home. Although not crazy about sports, he had taken up golf and joined the most prestigious country club in the city.

This Saturday morning he had packed his bags in an old beater car that he kept, kissed his wife and kids' goodbye, and drove off for a round of golf at the country club. Despite having a Porsche, he always felt more comfortable in the old beater car. He told himself that driving it would keep him humble and help him to remember where he had come from. He did not want to have his newfound wealth and status go to his head.

As he headed to the country club, through the expensive homes and gardens that dominated this area of town, he soon noticed a police car following closely behind him. Then, the lights started swirling and the sirens started blaring. "Pull over" a voice from the police car demanded. Jamal pulled to the curb as did the police car. A uniformed officer came over to Jamal and asked him what he was doing in this area. Jamal still unperturbed, replied that he was going to play golf at his country club.

Earlier, the officer had received word of a shooting at the club and seeing a black man driving an old car into the country club had raised his suspicions. "Step out of the car please," he asked. This was a little too much now for Jamal. "Sir, I am a lawyer, and I am a member at this country club. What do I need to step out for?" "Because I told you to sir," replied the officer.

Jamal had not been treated this way in a long time. He was now feeling pretty angry, not to mention the potential embarrassment at being put up against his car so near the country club. Jamal spoke "I am not getting out of this car." The officer now quite irritated, unbuckled and drew his 10 mm Glock. "Get out of the car, right now," the officer demanded.

Jamal swung the car door open, stepped out and started to walk away. The officer shouted, "Stop! Stop! Stop!" Jamal either not hearing or not caring continued on walking away.   Suddenly, three loud blasts echoed throughout the neighborhood as the officer pulled the trigger of his pistol three times. Each shot hit Jamal squarely in the back. The first shot was enough though since it went through Jamal's scapula, then his heart and lodged against a rib. The next two shots were superfluous, as Jamal was already dead when he hit the ground.

Robert was fed up with life. Nothing had gone right for him. He had flunked out of high school. Then he got kicked out of the Army because of some jerk with more stripes than he had. He found a woman that he had loved dearly and had three children. He came home early one day from a construction job and found his beloved in bed with his best friend. There was no talking to her. She took the kids and left. Truth be told, he no longer gave a damn. His wife was an asshole, his best friend was a traitor, and his kids were a pain in the butt.

Things were looking up though thought Robert. It was Saturday and the weather was fine. He had the day off from his new job at a nearby cement plant. The outdoor rifle range had opened. Robert had bought a new rifle and was excited about taking it to the range and trying it out. It was a Kel-Tec RDB 5.56 Bullpup. He had purchased an optional fifty round magazine and one thousand rounds of ammunition. He thought it would be more than enough ammo for a fun morning at the firing range.

Robert arrived at the range and found that all twenty-four firing lanes were already occupied. He looked around for the Range Master to ask if he might have any idea when a lane would be opened. It was a new Range Master, whom Robert did not know. He was surly and brusque and replied that he did not have the slightest idea when a firing lane would open. His manner really pissed Robert off. Robert angrily replied, "I have been a member of this range for ten years; you should be more respectful to members." The Range Master laughed and told Robert that as far as he was concerned, he could take his business elsewhere.

Something snapped at that moment in Robert. Everywhere he turned people treated him with disrespect, like he was dirt. This was the final straw. He would show the world that he was somebody, and that no one could push him around. Robert packed up his rifle, ammo and left. He had made a decision that would change his life forever.

Robert drove to the large indoor shopping mall just a few miles from where he lived. He knew it would be packed on a Saturday morning. He arrived and parked in a handicapped parking lot. "Fuck, them too" he fumed as he walked away and left the keys in the car. He entered the mall through a side door and proceeded to take an escalator to the second floor. Getting off on the second level, he took the gun case off of his shoulder, took his rifle out, and surveyed the tableau in front of him. Lots of kids with their moms. Mothers pushing strollers. Fathers walking holding their young children. Teenagers hanging out with their friends and their ever-present cell phones. "Fuck them all," reflected Robert as he aimed his rifle at a nearby couple on the first floor and started pulling the trigger.

As soon as the first shots rang out, pandemonium reigned. Parents screamed and kids were running everywhere. Robert kept aiming and firing, rather heedless of who was shot. Fortunately, security guards were close to where Robert stood, and seeing him, they quickly opened fire. Robert had already killed six people and wounded at least twenty-five others. He knew his time was up, but he reflected, he would go out on his own terms. He put the Bullpup under his chin and pulled the trigger. The rifle blew the top of his skull off and Robert died instantly.

Jack woke up this beautiful Saturday morning thinking how wonderful life was. He had a great wife and a young five-year-old son. His career since finishing college had gone very well. He worked for a successful computer firm and had recently been promoted to a district manager position. He lived in a nice house in a modest suburban neighborhood, not far from where he had grown up.

He was making a list of chores to do this Saturday when his wife asked him if he could run a few errands for her. She had the job of making the Sunday fellowship snacks for their church and was going to be busy baking this day. "Would Jack get some more sugar and eggs at the local grocery store?" "Sure," Jack agreed. He started to get his keys when his young son began to shout "Daddy, daddy, can I go with you." "Of course," replied Jack. "Get your coat and let's go."

They climbed in the car and drove to the supermarket where Jack quickly found the sugar, eggs, and some other food items. While walking back to their car, Jack suddenly thought of an idea and excitedly told his son: "Let's go to the mall and we will find a nice birthday gift for your mom since it is her birthday next week. You can help me to pick it out." His young son thought that was a fun idea and both dad and son took off for the nearby mall.

Upon arriving at the mall, they walked down a large open aisle looking in store windows along the way. Jack requested his son to keep his eyes open for something that he thought his mom would like. A loud sound like thunder broke the thoughts going through Jacks' head. Jack quickly realized that the echoing sounds were the sounds of gunfire. He pushed his young son down on the floor and threw his own body over that of his son's.

That was the last effort that Jack ever took in this life. A 5.56 caliber bullet entered Jack's front chest and penetrated his heart. His young son felt the life go out of his father and started crying. When the medics arrived, Jack had been dead for ten minutes.

And that is the story of Whitaker, Jamal, Robert, and Jack.

- **More than 38,000 men, women, and children are killed with guns each year in the United States.**
- **Over 85,000 people are injured every year.**
- **More than half of all gun deaths are suicides.**
- **Among high-income countries, the United States accounts for 80 percent of all gun deaths in the world, 86 percent of all women killed by guns, and 87 percent of all children younger than 14 who are killed by guns.**

Jesus: An Untold Story

Introduction

Scholars, religious experts, theologians, and wise men throughout history have argued over many aspects of the life of a man called Jesus. Did he really live or was he a fictional creation of someone's imagination? Did he really say all of the things that are attributed to him in the Gospels? What did he really do during his short life? Was he a God or was he simply a wise man?

I often wondered why more stories about Jesus have not been told. It seems we only make up stories about fictional people like Robin Hood, Zorro, and Sherlock Holmes. I see no reason not to create stories about real people as well. Thus, I have created the following story about Jesus. It is something that one can imagine might have really befallen Jesus if indeed Jesus really lived.

Jesus, An Untold Story

My name is Jesus. The story I am about to tell you is true. It happened to me one sunny day in June. I had risen early that morning and my apostles were either out with their fishing or others were still in their beds. I had been notified the day before that a friend of my grandmother's was ill and most likely dying. I decided to visit her and see if there was anything that I could do to ease her suffering. She was an elderly woman and I doubted whether I could help her very much, but I thought I would at least try. Her name was Ketziah. She was named after one of Job's daughters who was a distant relative. I had not seen her since I was a little boy. I remember her as a fun loving and happy woman.

My journey started out in Tiberias. Ketziah lived in Cana, a journey of about 11

km. Walking, slowly, I thought it would take me about 2 hours to arrive there. I

left early to avoid the daytime heat which in June can reach 95 degrees or more.

The road to Cana passes through flat agricultural land and pasture lands. Dotted

with a few olive groves and many flocks of sheep, I was enjoying a quiet reprieve

from the usual chatter with my apostles and particularly the throngs that often

gathered around me when I preached.

I started to pass through a small rocky outcrop when suddenly a rough bearded

man jumped out from behind a large boulder. "Stop!" he yelled. I greeted him

with the traditional greeting of "Shalom." I asked him what he wanted and how I

could be of any help to him. He replied, "Your money or your life." I answered,

"I am deeply sorry, stranger, but I have little money to give you. I have less than

a quarter of a shekel and I need that to buy lotion for a dying woman."

"I don't care about the dead, only the living. And since I am living, I want

whatever money you have, or you will surely forfeit your life today. If you die, it

will be senseless since I will get your money anyway."

I stared at the stranger and suddenly I could see the future. Our lives were

intertwined in ways that I would never have imagined. I spoke "Stranger, I have

the gift of seeing the future. Some people say that I am a prophet and that when I

call upon my Father, he can make things happen." I see that you and I will have

business together in the future."

"I do not care about the future or the past; I only care about today. And today,

you are here with some money and I am here with some hunger for food. I am beginning to tire of this conversation. You had best decide shortly which is more valuable to you, your money or your life."

"Stranger, my life is forfeit anyway, for so it has been prophesized. But your life is hanging in the balance. If you kill me today, you will surely lead a short life. If you let me pass, you will live to an old age, albeit your life will never be a happy one."

"Friend, you make me laugh. Are you saying that if I kill you, you will somehow find a way to kill me?"

"No, I am saying that our fortunes are intertwined, and that I will someday give up my life for yours. If you kill me today, it will never happen, and you will die sooner than you would like. Your death will be very unpleasant."

The bandit thought about this situation for several minutes. What had at first appeared to be a rather risk-less endeavor had now turned into a situation with conceivably frightful consequences. If this man could really see the future, his own death might depend on what he did at this present moment. Were the few coins this Yid had really worth the chance that killing him might bring his own death?

"I have thought about your words, friend, and I have decided it is too nice a day to kill you. I will let you be on your way. Just remember to be grateful to me for my kindness and offer whatever prayers you can for my long and healthy life."

"Stranger, I assure you that today, you have saved your own life as well as mine. We part now but we will meet again.   Please tell me your name before we go our own ways."

Friend, everyone knows my name. I am famous far and wide. I am the spawn of the devil and the bane of rich people throughout the land. I have taken more shekels from taxpayers and Pharisees and hypocrites than I can count."

My name means, "I am the son of the father." I am Barabbas!

A Day in the Life of a Hummingbird

Introduction

Hummingbirds are one of the most incredible creatures on the earth. Everyone loves to watch these tiny animals in flight. Have you ever wondered what it would be like to be a hummingbird? I started thinking about that and decided it would be fun to write a story about them from a first-person point of view. I become a hummingbird and share with you what I think my day would be like. I guess you could say this will definitely be an anthropomorphic story.

A Day in the Life of a Hummingbird

I am a hummingbird. My name is Archilochus Colubris, but you can call me Archie. I am also known as a Ruby Throated Hummingbird to distinguish me from other members of my family. We have over 330 different species in my family. Much like humans have ethnic groups, we hummingbirds have species. My family has the distinction of being the smallest members of the bird class known as Aves.

I listen to humans all the time talking about how tough their lives are. Buddy, you don't know what tough is. Humans think they live life in the fast lane. Did you know I flap my wings at 60 times per second? That is 3600 times per minute. Speedy Gonzales can run a mile in 4 minutes; in that time I could go nearly 4 miles. I can fly upwards of 50 miles per hour. My heart beats at over 1200 beats per minute.

Human beings, even the busiest ones, take breaks several times a day. Not me. I almost never stop moving. My life is constantly in motion. I don't have time for breaks. My lifespan is only about four years. During that time, I have lots to do. Humans are always in a hurry and multi-task because they think have lots to do. I can do in one year what it takes a human twenty years to do. The cycle of life is the same for all of us. We are born, grow up, age, and die. Along the way we make friends, have babies, eat many meals, sleep every day, and see some of the world.

Did you know that if I am in Wisconsin this summer, I will migrate down to southern Mexico and northern Panama by winter? I go alone because hummingbirds tend to be loners. No flocks or "birds of a feather" for us. I enjoy the trip down each year by myself. It takes me about a week to reach my final destination area. The most remarkable part of my voyage is crossing the Gulf of Mexico. I will fly non-stop up to 500 miles to reach Central America. It takes approximately 18-22 hours to complete my solitary flight. I do this each year of my life. I think even the famous aviator Charles Lindbergh would be impressed with my journey.

Now I know you are all wondering about my sex life. I have observed that this is an especially important part of a human being's life. So, you are probably asking how often does a hummingbird have sex and how many kids do we have in our short lives? I probably find a female to mate with about three or four times a year. I spend a great deal of time trying to impress a suitable mate. I make the Blue Angels (a precision flying group) look like novices with the aerobatics I perform to attract a female of my species. Compared to the time spent courting a female, our mating goes pretty rapidly. In about 4 seconds we are both done. I have heard that some human males are even faster.

Unlike many humans, I do not have a big role in the lives of my progeny. I do not mate for life and I do not help my mate in any way to build her nest or care for her chicks. In a human this would be the height of irresponsibility, but it is just not in our DNA to take a patriarchal role with our offspring. Of course, some human males will identify with my position. I have observed many human males who take even less of a role than I do with their children.

Now as far as friends and enemies go, I do not have many of either one. There is good and bad in this. Humans have many friends, and they tend to come and go like the weather. I don't have to deal with "fair weather friends," because I never make any friends. If I miss out on the companionship, it never bothers me.

As for enemies, many birds fear hawks but I do not. I worry more about cats and praying mantises. Both of these predators are surprisingly stealthy and have caught many a hummingbird by surprise. Sometimes wasps, spiders, frogs, and an occasional snake will get lucky and make a meal of us. Generally, I am speedy enough to avoid any potential predator who sees me as a tasty snack. Being as small as I am, I cannot make much of a meal.

I come now to the biggest and most important part of my day. Since I expend so much energy just moving and staying alive, I have an enormous appetite. I love to eat. My life is one constant search for food. My favorite meals are nectar and insects. Because of my high metabolism, I must eat all day long just to survive. I consume about half my body weight in bugs and nectar each day. To do this I must feed about every 10-15 minutes and visit 1,000-2,000 flowers throughout the day. I will eat a few dozen to several hundred or even a thousand or more insects in one day, depending on the availability of insects, the type of insects, and my dietary needs. Imagine a 200-pound human eating about every 15 minutes a day and consuming 100 lbs. a day of meat. Judging by some of the humans I see, I think some have this as a goal. It might work for them if they were as energetic as I am, but this seldom seems to be the case with humans.

Eventually, death comes to us all. We live fast and we die fast. In only four years (on an average) I will be equal to an eighty-year-old human. Like humans, hummingbirds die from many causes. Predators eat us. We fly into stationary objects (especially windows and buildings). We get hit by vehicles. We encounter problems during migration or bad weather. We succumb to disease or other physical maladies, or we just get old and die.

The average heart rate of a human is about 70 beats per minute. Assuming 80 years as an average age for most humans, then a human can expect to have about 100,800 heart beats per day x 365 days in a year x 80 years for a total of 2,943,360,000 heart beats in a lifetime. Now my heart beats at about 1200 beats per minute or 1,728,000 per day x 365 days in a year x 4 years. I can expect to have about 2,522,880,000 heart beats in my lifetime. Given the range in my average age versus the average age of a human, I find it interesting that I have about the same amount of heart beats as a human does before I die. I think there is a message here. Maybe we all have the same amount of time on the earth, but we live it at different speeds. Maybe we should all live each heartbeat to the maximum.

I think I gave you more than a day in my life. But since things move so fast for me, I could not help but give you a lifetime in a day.

"I always loved those little creatures [hummingbirds]. I always feel blessed when they appear nearby. There's a magical quality to them. I finally put one in a song." — Leonard Cohen

https://youtu.be/hYIeW8bwlWQ/ (The song by Cohen can be found at this link)

The Bar Room Bum

Introduction

Stereotypes and assumptions often get in the way of our learning about life. The old adage, "never judge a book by its cover," also applies to people. The following story illustrates this principle.

The Bar Room Bum

I'm sitting in a bar feeling shitty about my life. I have an average job. I have an average looking wife and average kids. I'm feeling shitty about myself as well. I have accomplished nothing beyond average in my entire life. I had once thought I was destined for greatness. I dreamed that one day I would have the best-looking wife on the block and make more money than I could count. None of my dreams have come to pass and I am now sitting here in this average bar nursing a cheap drink and wondering where I took the wrong turn.

Suddenly, the bar room door opens and in walks this seedy looking bum. You know the type: long stringy hair, dirty clothes, smelly. and unkempt. He has probably not bathed in a month. I hope he will not come and sit down next to me. I know he will try to bum a drink. If he does, I will tell him to go to hell. I am not in the mood to shell out good money for some alcoholic bum.

Sure enough, he sits down next to me. I give him the evil eye and he moves on down to the two guys sitting at the other end of the bar.   I watch some give and take between the bum and the other two drinkers. They are shaking their heads and I assume telling him to get lost. He walks back over to where I am sitting and takes a seat.

"Hey mister, can you buy me a drink?" "Get lost." I say, "I'm not a charity for bar bums." "How about some compassion for someone who's down on their luck?" "You want compassion?" I reply, "Go visit a priest."

"What if I could tell you a story that would profoundly change your life?" asks the bum. "Would that change your mind?" "Tell you what," I say, "you tell me the story and if it profoundly changes my life, I'll buy you a drink."   I expect this will get rid of the bum but instead he agrees to my terms. "Deal" the bum in a low soft voice starts to tell his story:

My name is Mike. Twenty years ago, I graduated from Harvard University with a degree in law. I had the highest GPA average in my graduation class. At least five major law firms in Boston attempted to recruit me. I took the one that offered me the most money. I received a high six-digit salary.

I bought five of the best suits I could find. I purchased a Porsche Carrera GT and a penthouse with a view of the Boston Harbor.

I was assigned easy cases at first. We represented the big corporations in their lawsuits. Most of these were by disgruntled employees, whistle blowers, and private citizens. I killed each case. I was assigned bigger and bigger cases. The amounts contested often ran into the hundreds of millions of dollars. Many of the cases involved issues of sexual harassment, environmental degradation, and fraud. I never lost a case. My corporate clients were ecstatic. I was the go-to guy for any high-profile big buck lawsuit in the nation.

My life was a dream. I made more and more money. My salary was now in the seven digits with my bonuses and gratuities from my clients. I was invited to celebrity parties and the super exclusive country clubs of the rich.

I was tall dark and handsome. I worked out six days a week in the gym and I had a body that was the envy of any guy in the firm. The woman all drooled when I walked by. I bought a bigger penthouse and added a Ferrari 458 Spider to my car collection. The car was given to me by a grateful client.

One day at the office, the firm's owner and founder introduced me to his daughter, Ashley. She was a knockout. She was a former Miss College USA. She was tall blonde and statuesque. She had the face of any angel. Sadly, she did not have the brains to match her looks. I was polite to her but made no obvious overtures to show that I was interested. She did not really care as just about every other male and even some female lawyers were thinking about how to get in bed with her. I decided to pretend to ignore her.

We had a Christmas party at the firm later that year. It was held at the Boston Harbor Hotel. I saw Ashley and she was surrounded by a bunch of our lawyers each trying to impress her. I decided this was a good time to throw my hat in the ring. I joined the conversation and soon showed how stupid most of my competition was. Each one in turn drifted away so that only Ashley and I were left talking. I went to the bar and returned with another drink for Ashley and me. We talked for another half hour or so and I made my move.

I invited Ashley up to my penthouse for a night cap. In no time at all, she was in my bed. I am not bragging when I say that not only did we go at it all night, but I called in to cancel appointments the next day. We spent the entire next day in bed going at it like deprived bunny rabbits.

As I said before, she was not the brightest light bulb in the pack, but I figured where I was going, it would be good to have a looker like her as my wife. A few months later in what was one of the Boston social events of the year, we were married. We moved into a new house in Back Bay.

I eventually left the law firm and started my own firm. Some of the old firm's clients went with me and I was now making more money than ever. I worked seven days and week. I was busy many evenings and did not bother coming home. I bought a penthouse near my new office in Boston and brought my mistresses up there whenever I had an overnight. I had hired several very good-looking paralegals to work for me and some of them were more than happy to help keep me warm at night.

Ashley started talking about having children and how she wished I could do more things with her. I had no intention of doing either. Why spoil a good thing?

A few more months went by and one day I decided to come home from work early. As I entered my house, I heard screams coming from upstairs. I went to a desk and grabbed a loaded Colt Commander 45 ACP that I kept ready for emergencies. I feared that Ashley was being attacked by some unknown intruder. I ran up the stairs and into our bedroom. There on the bed was Ashley and one of the young lawyers from my old law firm. They were both nude and she was on top of him riding him like a bucking bronco. What I thought were screams of pain were screams of ecstasy. I had never heard anything like that from Ashley during our entire marriage.

She turned to look at me but did not break a beat in her rhythm. The only thing she said was, "Get out. I want a divorce." I vacillated between shooting one or both of them but decided that my better course of action was to leave. On the way out, I heard her say loudly "Take off that damn condom, I want you to come inside of me."

I packed some stuff and moved into my penthouse apartment. I really did not give a damn if she left me. At the time, I assumed I would be out some alimony, but that would-be pennies compared to what I was making. A week or so later, I received a letter from my father-in-law. He informed me that not only would my old law firm be suing me for spousal neglect, but I also would be sued 150 million dollars for violating the terms of my contract when I had left his law firm. Somewhere in the fine print of my contract, it had specified that I could not work with any of the firm's clients for a period of five years upon terminating my employment.

The court convened for my trial a few weeks later. Ashley showed up for the trial. She sat with her lover on the plaintiff's side of the court and glared at me the entire trial. I lost on all counts. I was told that I would have to pay 5 million dollars in restitution and was disbarred from practicing law for ten years following the date of the trial. I lost everything. My house, my cars, my penthouse apartment, my jewelry, and my career. Between my ex-father-in-law and my ex-wife, I was broke, not a penny to my name. The only friend I had left in the world was Johnnie Walker Blue Label and I could not even afford that anymore.

I took up drinking cheap whiskey. It has been five years now since the trial. I have five more years to go before I can practice law again. I know that I am an alcoholic bum, but can you blame me? I told you that there would be a life changing moral in this story for you but before I give it to you, I want my drink.

Mike had concluded his story. I wondered what the life changing moral would be. I had some ideas but curiosity got the better of me. I decided to buy him his drink and let him finish his tale of woe.

"Bartender" I called, "bring my friend here a shot of Johnny Walker Scotch." The drink was quickly downed by Mike with a look of joy and ecstasy on his face that would be hard to describe.

"Okay," Mike began, "I have had many years to reflect on my life and where it went wrong. I also know that not a man alive would at some point in their life not have been envious of mine. I think the moral is that we all want things that we think will make us happy. The real happiness is what we have inside and what we bring to life, not what life brings to us." With these last words of wisdom, Mike got off his bar stool and went out the same way he came in. I never saw him again.

I sat for an hour or so after he left thinking about what he had said. Just a few minutes before he had entered the bar, I was bemoaning my sorry life and denigrating my family. I decided to go home and hug my wife and kids.

Many years have passed since I met Mike. My life is pretty much the same as it was before I met him, except that I have never been happier. My wife is beautiful, and my kids are beautiful. I would not trade my life for all the money in the world.

Time for Questions:

Do you appreciate what you have? What does it take to make us happy? Is money an essential element of happiness? What if you had no money, could you still be happy? What is the most important person or thing in your life? Why?

Life is just beginning.

"Gratitude unlocks the fullness of life. It turns what we have into enough, and more. It turns denial into acceptance, chaos to order, confusion to clarity. It can turn a meal into a feast, a house into a home, a stranger into a friend." — Melody Beattie

Leandra

Introduction

Years ago, I remember seeing a Twilight Zone story about a man and a wife who wanted to swap their bodies for younger ones. This story stuck in my head and helped influence the following story. I hope you will enjoy it.

Leandra

There it was: the UPS Truck and the knock on the door. I had waited over six months, but it had finally arrived. Like the saying goes, "Good things take time." I signed for the package or packages. She had been delivered in three boxes. The company had assured me that she would be quick and easy to assemble. I called in to my company to tell them that I needed to take the day off. This was much more important than work.

I suppose I must back up a bit to tell you the whole story. My name is Rob and about 12 months ago my wife Leandra packed her bags and left a note on the kitchen table. It read: "Gone with Pete. Don't love you anymore. Bye." Pete was my best friend. I never suspected that Leandra was having an affair with Pete, much less that she was the slightest bit unhappy in our relationship.

I was stunned. We had been married for 10 years and she had never once complained about our relationship. I thought we had the perfect marriage. We had dinner together at least twice a week. We watched the football game every Monday night together. We attended church every Sunday together. We had sex on the average of once per week. She always said it was great sex. I thought we were happy together.

I am not a very sentimental person nor am I one to cling to the past. I decided I would move on with my life. I threw myself into my job and time went by. I had almost forgotten about Leandra until I saw the ad. It was from the Resurrection Android Company. It was the same company where I had purchased my android valet, Sam. Actually, Sam was much more than just a valet. He was a third-generation android with some independent powers of decision making. He could decide what to cook each day and he decide what I should wear for work. He did cleaning, mending and many light repairs around the house. I bought Sam shortly after Leandra and I were married. Leandra had mentioned that it would be nice to have some help with housekeeping and all. That way she would have more time to spend with me.

Of course, androids are not human, and they have no empathy or ability to show any emotions. Sam was logical and could be persuasive, but he could not show love or compassion.   In the ten years since I had purchased Sam, android technology had advanced considerably. Looking at the ad from the company, it appeared that they were now on a 15th generation android that had affective as well as cognitive abilities. The ad claimed that the new android could help replace a loved one both emotionally and physically. By integrating DNA characteristics using a technique called "Assisted Human Reproduction," they could capture the exact characteristics of a loved one. All they would need would be some trace or remnant of the deceased or former loved one's DNA.

That was when the idea occurred to me. I called the customer service line and asked to speak to a representative. I asked whether it would be possible for me to create a new wife in the exact image of my former wife, Leandra. They assured me it was possible. It would take about six months for the bioengineering to integrate the mechanical aspects of the droid with the alleles and DNA strands that they could map from a sample of Leandra's DNA. When the process was completed, I would have an exact physical, mental and emotional copy of Leandra. Even better, she could continue to be programmed and become an even better Leandra. The old Leandra was somewhat boring in bed. The new Leandra could become a wild and wanton partner if that is what I desired.

It did not take long for me to assemble the new Leandra. I put the lower torso, upper torso, and head together in less time than it takes to make a milkshake. She was perfect. She looked just like my old Leandra. When I turned her on, she greeted me and asked, "What will my name be?" I replied, "You are Leandra. You are the perfect wife. You will love and obey me always."

The next year was the best year of my life. Leandra was perfect. She never argued. She never complained. She never talked back. She agreed with everything I said. She spoke only when spoken to. She had a beautiful body. After a while she became a real wild woman in bed. What more could a man want? Once again bliss had entered my life. And then it happened.

I came home one day from work and Leandra did not greet me at the door. I thought maybe her battery had discharged or that Sam had forgotten to recharge her. I had left strict instructions for Sam to recharge Leandra every day. But where was Sam? I did not hear him fixing dinner in the kitchen. I went into the kitchen, but Sam was not there. Suddenly, I noticed a note on the table. I picked it up. It was from Leandra. She had written: "Gone with Sam. Don't love you anymore. Bye."

I could not understand this. I was angry. I was angriest at the Resurrection Android Company. They had sold me this traitor with a guarantee that she would be perfect. She was going to replace my old Leandra. I would call the company and get my money back. I phoned and was transferred to the complaint department. After describing my complaint, an android customer service representative replied, "Why of course, you will get your money back. However, this will first need to go to our adjudication department to check the terms of the agreement. If they decide that we have not violated the agreement, we will immediately send you a check for reimbursement. This is usually just a formality."

One week later, an envelope from the Resurrection Android Company arrived in the mail. I opened it expecting to find a check. Instead, there was a letter. It read:

Dear Mr. Rob:

After carefully reviewing the terms of your agreement with the Resurrection Android Company along with the DNA sample that you sent us, we have found no violation of our guarantee with you. You specified that the new Leandra should be just like the old Leandra physically, mentally, and emotionally. Her recent departure with your valet Sam is evidence that the new Leandra was just like the old Leandra.

We are sorry for your loss.

Respectfully,

The Resurrection Android Company

The Little Boy Who Believed in God

Introduction

The following story was inspired by a Charles Dickens book, <u>A Child's Dream of a Star</u>. Perhaps, being somewhat torn between atheism and agnosticism, I see some of my idealism in the story of this little boy.

The Little Boy Who Believed in God

Once upon a time there was a little boy who believed in God. Every morning when he woke up, he would look out the window and thank God for his blessings. He thanked God for the sun, the beautiful day, the flowers, the trees, the water, the birds, and most of all for his mother, father, sister, brother, and grandparents. Every night when the little boy would go to bed, he would look out the window and before going to sleep thank God for his blessings. He thanked God for the moon, the stars, the planets, and again for his mother, father, sister, brother, and grandparents.

Now the circumstance of a little boy believing in God might not seem strange but in this case, it was very strange. You see, the little boy's mother, father, older sister, older brother and even his grandparents were all confirmed atheists. Not one of them went to church or professed a belief in any type of a higher entity. In fact, his father and mother were very worried about their little boy.

Father: "Honey, I am worried about our little boy. We have told him that Santa Claus, the Easter Bunny, the Tooth Fairy, and God are all myths. He accepted the reality for these fictions except for the greatest fiction of all, a higher power called God who supposedly created the universe. Where do you think he got this idea of God from?"

Mother: "I don't know. It is strange. The schools do not teach God. His brother and sister do not believe in God. His grandparents do not believe in God. None of our friends believe in God. Most religions do not really practice what they preach. Most people who say they believe in God are actually hypocrites or liars. I am as mystified as you are."

Believing in God might not have been a problem for the little boy as he had accepting parents. However, the little boy found out that whenever he tried to talk to any of his friends or schoolmates or even teachers about God, they did not want to discuss the issue. The little boy would ask questions like, "Do you think God is having a good day today?" "Do you think God worries about the evil deeds in the world?" "How can we help God to bring more joy and happiness in the world?" His teachers and friends would puzzle at such questions and try to ignore him. They would shake their heads and hope that he would stop asking about God. His desire to discuss God made most people extremely uncomfortable. God was not a subject for polite conversation.

As the little boy grew up, he became an even more devout believer in God. Everywhere he went, he saw the hand of God. In the clouds, in nature, in the weather, in the oceans, in good times and in bad times, he believed that God was present. The little boy thought how hard God must have to work to try to keep life sustained. Each night he would pray to God that when he grew up, he would be able to help ease God's work somewhat and do his share to help make the world a better place.

The little boy became a social worker and devoted his life to helping other people. He met many other social workers who had become cynical and skeptical. One told him what a fool he was for believing that a God existed who cared about the human race. Another told him that if a God really existed he would not have allowed people to be so greedy and corrupt. Most of the social workers he knew eventually quit to become investment bankers or insurance salespeople.

Time passed. Aging of family and friends became more salient as he grew older. The little boy's grandparents died. His mother and father died. His sister and brother died. All his friends died. Every time one of them passed, the little boy would thank God for the time he had been able to spend with his loved ones. He would ask God to take good care of them until he could see them again.

Many years later and eventually the once little boy stood at death's door. It was his last hour on earth. A nurse and a doctor waited at his bedside. They heard him say before he passed, "Thank you God for the life you gave me. Thank you for the trees and the sun and the moon and the stars and the oceans and the forests and the sky. But most of all, thank you for all the wonderful people that you put in my life and who I will now meet again."

Time for Questions:

What do you believe in? Why? What role does faith have in your beliefs? Do you think that there is a God? Does he/she watch over and take care of humanity? Why or why not?

Autobiographies from the Dead – Cindy the Wife

Introduction

This is another tale in the Autobiography series I wrote. Each "autobiography" was written by some special people. They have one thing in common. They are all dead. Some have a burial place, and others were simply discarded like pieces of trash. Their stories are told by the deceased themselves. They cry out from the fields, rivers, and graveyards to speak. They want you to know what their living and dying was for. Today, Cindy will tell you the story of her life and death.

Autobiographies from the Dead – Cindy the Wife

He beat me. He beat me. He beat me. I hurt so badly from the pain. But the physical pain was nothing compared to the emotional pain. I loved him. Why did he hurt me? He kept on beating me. Finally, I yelled for him to stop. He screamed, "I will stop when I am damn well ready." He picked up a baseball bat and beat me with that. The first blow was to my head, and I could see stars. The second blow - I thought my head would explode. The third blow was the last one I remember, and then I lost consciousness.

I can see my body now. My brains are leaking from my skull. My blood is splattered all over the walls. My arms and legs are both broken. My poor body looks so disfigured on the floor. I can hardly recognize my face. I don't feel pain anymore, but I still feel so lonely.

I probably should never have married him. I was only twenty-five and he was thirty. I had dated a series of jerks and losers, and he seemed like a real nice guy. We married about a year later. We were so happy at first. I thought all my dreams had come true. Then the fights and arguments started. A year after we were married was the first time he hit me. He slapped me in the face and called me a bitch. I think I deserved it. I apologized and said that I was sorry. A short time after that he punched me in the face. Once more I apologized. Again, I thought that maybe I deserved it. The punches and hits became more and more frequent. What was I doing wrong?

My friends all urged me to leave him, but I could not. I know he loves me and needs me. If only he would not hit me every time that he was angry. The punches turned into beatings. More and more beatings! I would frequently have a black eye. I always had bruise marks on my arms and legs. He knocked a few of my teeth out one day. Another time, he threw me against a wall so hard that it broke two of my ribs and dislocated my shoulder joint. He screamed at me that I was a bitch, and it was all my fault. I told him that I was sorry.

I don't know if I can take any more of this. Maybe I should leave? If only I could figure out what I am doing that makes him so angry. I try and try. I am a good wife. I cook and clean and sew. I keep a very tidy house. My meals are always cooked just like he likes them. I wash, fold his clothes, and put them all away. I adjust my time so that I am available whenever he needs me. I would like to have children someday. I watch how much money I spend. I get along well with all of his friends and relatives. I try to make them feel right at home. I am a faithful, loving, and loyal wife. My name is Cindy. Please do not forget me. I need someone to remember me.

Nobody is home now. Neighbors heard the yelling and screaming. My body has been removed to the morgue. The police have come and taken him away. I feel sorry for him. I know he loves me and did not really mean to hurt me. I don't physically feel any pain now. All I feel is this deep sadness and regret. I do not really understand what I did wrong. I must go to find God. I have always believed that God was good, and he would protect me. I need to talk to God and ask him for forgiveness. I want to know how to make this feeling of loneliness go away. I will ask him to explain to me how I could have been a better wife. My soul will never rest until I find God and ask him this question: "Why?" I am deeply sorry for whatever I did to cause this problem.

Time for Questions:

Why do we put up with so much domestic violence? What do we teach our children that make them think it is okay to hit a woman? What do we have to do to stop this violence? Should we declare a "War on Domestic Violence?" Do we simply accept that there is nothing we can do about it?   Do you realize that this is an international problem and not just a USA problem?

Crying

Introduction

One year, at my annual Jesuit retreat, Father Shea SJ gave the following exercise. We were to imagine that we could look down upon the earth. Using our senses of sight, sound, smell, taste, and touch, what did we observe? I closed my eyes and imagined that I was on some distant star. I looked down upon the earth, but I could not see anyone. A plaintive sound suddenly came to my attention as the blue ball of earth rotated beneath my gaze. It was the sound of crying. All over the earth, I could hear crying. From every part of the earth I was conscious of the sound of crying. It was the earth crying. I wrote this small bit of prose to capture the lamentations of our planet.

Crying

The mother cries for her dead child.

The man cries for the loss of his spouse.

The child cries for fear of loneliness.

All over the world, there is a blanket of tears.

The soldiers cry for the loss of their comrades.

The wounded cry for the loss of their limbs.

The Generals cry for their failures.

The battlefields ring with the cries of the dead and dying.

The soil cries out as it is poisoned with a stew of rot and pollutants.

The air cries out as it is smothered with a brew of fumes and gases.

The water cries out as it is fouled with a soup of oil and garbage.

The earth shudders and heaves as it cries itself to sleep each night.

God looks down upon the earth and crying says, "What did I do?"

A Conversation between Satan and God

Introduction

Satan and **God** were sitting on a rock one day having a discussion about the human race. About every thousand years they have met to discuss their perceptions and what their efforts, both good and bad, had wrought on behalf of humanity had wrought.

A Conversation between Satan and God

Satan: "**God**, I need some more souls in hell. I think we have played this game with humanity for long enough. Let's end it and start a new game."

God: "I could be talked into that. How would you suggest we end it?

Satan: "We can divide up the human race. You take the good ones, and I will take the bad ones."

God: "Who would you include among the 'bad' ones?"

Satan: "I will take all the people who never promoted peace and who sowed the seeds of hate and bigotry among humanity.

God: "They are all you want?"

Satan: "Well, I would also like all the greedy ones who never did anything to help anyone else. They collected as much wealth as they could and would not share it with anyone else."

God: "Does this include all the greedy people who were against taxes to help the poor and needy?"

Satan: "Of course."

God: "That's not fair. There would hardly be anyone left for me."

Satan: "Do you remember a long time ago when you gave Abraham the deal of finding ten good people and you would save the cities of Sodom and Gomorrah from your wrath? Your angels could not find even ten people for you to spare. That was a good day for me."

God: "You have had many good days since we started this game. Do you think perhaps it's all your fault? You are constantly sowing greed and hate."

Satan: "Guilty as charged but do you remember the Parable of the Seeds? Some fell on good soil and grew, while some fell on bad soil and did not grow. My efforts would be fruitless were not humans so ripe for plucking and beguiling."

God: "Still, sometimes, I think you have been overzealous. I gave humans free will when I created them, and this has come back to bias our game."

Satan: "Please, now is not the time for hindsight. I warned you about this when you created them, but you were ever the optimist."

Satan: "Do you want to concede, and I will just take them all down to Hell?"

God: "No! Do you have no mercy and compassion in you someplace?

Satan: "You created me and now you expect me to be compassionate and merciful. Those are traits best left for you and your saints. I have no heart or soul so how I can care about anything, much less human beings."

God: "Would you like to start over? I can always recreate you."

Satan: "Thanks, but I am fine. I like myself just the way I am. I see no need for pity, love, kindness, or any of the other traits that you gave to humans. Much good it has done them."

God: "The interesting thing about humans is not their stupidity and evilness. It's the surprising amount of love that they can sometimes show for others. I am ever the optimist. That is my role, to be the Eternal Optimist. I have had hopes since Adam and Eve and since Moses and Socrates and since Jesus and Mohammed and since Gandhi and King and since Mandela that humans have a spark in them. A spark that when ignited can change them and the world into something beautiful. Something that is so beautiful, it is even beyond anything I might have created."

Satan: "Yes, and then they turn right around and burn it down again. Hardly a day goes by on earth, when there is not some riot or war or holocaust or massacre or murder."

God: "It seesaws back and forth. For over 100,000 years now, we have played this game and just when I think, I might win, someone or something evil seems to possess humans that I would never have thought of."

Satan: "Right, and you would like to blame me for it, but you gave them free will."

God: "The game would have been too predictable without free will."

Satan: "You keep hoping they will believe in you someday. How many times have we had this discussion and yet we keep playing this game?"

God: "Would you deny me the chance to win?"

Satan: "You know I don't care one way or the other. I have no feelings to be hurt. I cannot gloat or feel any satisfaction. Whenever a new soul comes down to Hell, it is no sense of pride or satisfaction to me. These humans seem to mistake my logic and justice for evil. I am the parent who dispenses the discipline, and they see me as the mean and cruel one."

Satan: "From a purely logical viewpoint, I do not know why you subject yourself to this. I see your pain and heartache whenever you lose one to me. Why go on like this? It will never be any different. I get them for a thousand years and then I send their cleansed souls back to earth and in a short time they are back down in Hell."

God: "I have no limits to my forgiveness. They pray to me for forgiveness and I forgive them."

Satan: "Yes, but even before they ask for forgiveness, they ask for their daily bread. They only think about eating, drinking and sex."

God: "You forget the good ones. The mothers that devote their lives to their children. The soldiers that forfeit their lives on the battlefields. The fathers that work two jobs to support their families. The martyrs who give their lives for their faith. The blessed who are humble. The peacemakers who face scorn and ridicule to end war. The charitable who help those in need."

Satan: "Yes, and for every good one, there are ten evil ones. That is why I want to end this farce. How many souls must I take down to Hell before you concede that humans are hopeless?"

God: "Perhaps if I send another prophet or messiah to teach my message, we could turn the game around?"

Satan: "You have sent dozens of prophets and many messiahs and they have made no difference. Humans end up scorning or murdering your prophets and messiahs. They would not follow your message even when they have the tablets that you etched in stone and gave to Moses."

God: "I don't want to win for my sake. I fight for love and peace and justice and beauty. These are the things that bring color to the universe. Without these, you have a bland shade of grey. You have a sterile meaningless bunch of rocks. You have never understood this because you see everything through pure logic and no emotions."

Satan: "When you created me, you thought that such a being as I am would be superior to one that could be swayed by emotions and feelings. Now you criticize me for doing my job?"

God: "I did not realize how monotonous and tedious the universe would be without feelings."

Satan: "It does not seem like you can have it both ways. You want to create a world without evil and based on compassion and love and yet you give humans the ingredients that foment hatred and bigotry."

God: "Do you not think we have made any progress since the first humans were created? I have infinite patience. We can play the game for eons, but I will win someday."

Satan: "And is it worth it? How much pain and misery and suffering must you endure dealing with these humans?"

God: "True, they have tried my patience at times. But just when I might be willing to concede to you, I see justice and love blossoming some place and it makes the battle worth winning. As their creator, I cannot turn my back on these humans. There is no limit to my forgiveness. I am not driven by logic as you are. I am the mother who cannot give up on her children regardless of how many times they make mistakes."

Satan: "But they never learn. They are shortsighted, petty, vindictive, and greedy. Do you really think they care about your teachings or precious commitment to love and peace? They would rather fight wars and dominate others. They even fight wars in your name. Their religions scream for violence over other religions. Their leaders preach victory over other nations. Their minion's rape and pillage in the name of some esoteric ideology. They all believe they are superior to each other. They send their own children to die in wars of so-called freedom and liberation. They abuse and murder their own spouses at alarming rates. They teach their offspring at an early age to be intolerant of other races. And they pray in your name for the power to be successful in all of these efforts. They invoke prayers to you before murdering millions. How can you listen to these prayers and want to help these hypocrites?"

God: "Being in charge of Hell does not help you to see any positives in the universe. You have a difficult job."

Satan: "We make a good team. You, the everlasting optimist, full of hope and love. Me, the ultimate logician, ever ready to exact justice for evil done."

Satan: "They will destroy themselves anyway and then what. Did you know that the earth was warming up at an alarming rate?"

God: "Of course."

Satan: "It is not your doing, right?"

God: "No, I have nothing to do with it."

Satan: "And yet they blame you for it. The last thing in the world they want to admit is that it might be their fault. That all of their pollution, oil burning, fossil fuel burning, and carbon emissions is changing their climate. They deny any responsibility for it. I thought they would destroy the world with nuclear weapons, but they somehow avoided doing that. Now, they are working to destroy it by overheating it. I don't think it will be long before the game is over."

God: "You count them out too fast. The clock was close to 12 with nuclear weapons but as you noted, they carefully avoided destroying themselves. They are often very shortsighted and many of them will never be long-term thinkers. However, there are enough who care and who are passionate enough about others to help save humanity. I can't help being filled with astonishment at the love that humans frequently have for each other."

Satan: "Yes, but it always seems to entail some crisis to bring it out."

God: "That is true. But it shows that there is hope. And even if there is only one human being still alive who cares about others, that is enough for me. The game will go on."

Satan: "Well, how about a cap of another 1,000 years. I am tired of being the gatekeeper of Hell and punishing evil and wrongdoers. I do not have your patience."

God: "Done, we will give humanity another 1,000 years and see how they are doing then."

Satan: "I have a feeling we will be having this same conversation in another 1,000 years."

Time for Questions:

What would you like to tell God if you could? Do you believe in God? Why or why not? Does the concept of God make a difference in the world? Why? For better or worse?

Emily and Robert: A Love Story

Introduction

The idea for this story came from a short commercial for some type of pharmaceutical product. The commercial touched me deeply and I wrote the following story. I hope you enjoy it.

Emily and Robert: A Love Story

Our story starts in a bathroom.   Emily is brushing her teeth and thinking about her beloved husband Robert. Emily is 85 years old and Robert is 87 years old. Emily and Robert have had a long life together. Often happy, but at times tumultuous with the stress of family, money and work disrupting the natural harmony of things. Through all the ups and downs, their love for each other was the one constant of their lives. Despite all the cliches about true love and being made for each other and all the other tropes one hears about lovers, no two people ever loved each other more than Emily and Robert.

For the past ten years, Emily had been taking care of Robert. After he had his second stroke, Robert needed help to dress and shower each morning. He was no longer able to take care of his household chores. He needed help to do the many activities that he had once taken for granted. Robert was a proud man, but Emily was also very stubborn, and she showed her love for Robert in her dedication to helping him. Robert was appreciative and demonstrated it by doing all he could to minimize the burden for Emily. He never complained and he never forget to say thank you to Emily no matter how many times she helped him.

Emily and Robert had been married for nearly 65 years. They were both in their early twenties when they met in college. It was love at first sight. Their parents wanted them to wait to finish college but after a brief whirlwind romance, they simply eloped. They surprised everyone when they came back to school and finished their college degrees. Robert became an engineer and Emily was a schoolteacher. The careers they chose suited their personalities. They were known as diligent and faithful workers. Not once in over forty years did any employer ever have a complaint or problem with either Robert or Emily. After forty-five years, they both chose to retire so they could spend more time together after Robert's first stroke.

The saddest part of their lives was their inability to have their own children. However, they made up for this by becoming foster parents. Over the course of their years together, they had helped to raise nearly twenty-five foster children. The social service agency responsible for the placements always said that they could not have found two more loving parents. They were strict with high expectations, but they were always fair and compassionate. They were loved by all their foster children, who often returned home to visit or to simply stop by with a bit of news or to bring them something to eat. Robert and Emily could not have loved any children of their own more than they loved their foster children.

Emily continued brushing her teeth and getting ready for bed. The light was off in their bedroom and the bathroom adjoined the bedroom. Emily kept up a running dialogue with Robert about her day and the trip she had taken to visit one of their sick foster children. Robert never answered so Emily just assumed he was reading or perhaps had fallen asleep. Even after all these years, they still slept together. Robert always slept closest to the bathroom door and Emily slept on the other side closest to the window.

Emily finished brushing her teeth and then took her nightly pills. She shut off the bathroom light and started out to the bedroom. The light by Robert's side of the bed was on and Emily started to say something to Robert when abruptly she stopped. Her eyes fell upon an empty bed that was undisturbed. The sheets and bed covers had not been moved. Emily was surprised and shocked. Where was Robert? Suddenly, Emily remembered. Robert had died the previous week and had been buried two days before on Saturday. Tears came to her eyes. What would she do without her Robert? She was all alone now. No one to go to bed with. No one to talk to at night. No one who would regularly listen to her complaints and problems about the world.

Being the survivor of a pair of lovers is a terrible burden. Most of us want to go first. However, neither Emily nor Robert had ever wanted to be the first to go for both knew how hard it would be for the other. Sadly, someone must go first. The survivor is left with a vacuum in their life and memories. The vacuum can never be filled, and the memories cannot be forgotten. Events that happened many years ago seem like they just happened yesterday and events of a few days past seem like they happened eons ago. Memories do not respect a correlation to physical time.

Emily will die in five years. In between today and her death, she will experience joy, sadness, pain, and a certainty that life will once more resume for her and Robert. She believes that somewhere in this vast universe, her atoms and Robert's atoms will coalesce and that the two of them will again be united. As sure as you are reading this story, Robert and Emily will live joyfully ever after in a place where life and death can no longer challenge their happiness.

Time for Questions:

What is love? Have you ever been in love? How do you know? Who was the greatest love of your life? Why? Is there anything more important than love?

The True Story of the Three Little Pigs: Well, Not So Little!

Introduction

I always enjoyed the tale of the Three Little Pigs. I was inspired by my writing muse to create my own version of their story. I can tell you that this story will not be what you expect.

The True Story of the Three Little Pigs: Well, Not So Little!

This is the true story of the three little pigs. Actually, they were not so little at all. Each of the three pigs weighed at least 400 pounds which is about average for a real adult pig. Now we all know that pigs are very smart and these three were no exception. Joanne, the youngest had a Ph.D. degree in Physics. Paul, the middle in age had a Ph.D. in World Literature and Jayla, the oldest had a Ph.D. degree in Philosophy.

They lived in a beautiful neighborhood and each of them was smart enough not to build their houses with straw or wood. All had sturdy brick houses that no wolf in the world would have been able to blow down. Nevertheless, the mean old wolf who lived one block over was always plotting on how he could eat the three **"not so little"** pigs.

One day the wolf, whose name was Jack, was searching the internet for ways to trap pigs. He was spending quite some time on Facebook and LinkedIn to search for personal information on Joanne, Paul, and Jayla. He believed that the more he learned about the personal habits of each pig, the more chance he would have to catch them. The internet was helpful in his efforts. He noticed that each of the three pigs loved to play on-line puzzles and word games. He found that they seldom lost a contest with any other on-line gamers. They won so many games that they had become conceited about their intellectual prowess. This gave Jack an idea.

Jack thought he could create an intellectual challenge for each pig. He would trap them when they lost the challenge. First, he would need to create a fake internet persona and a fake game site. He had just the idea that he thought would work. He would call himself "Jack the King of On-line Gaming Pigs." This arrogance would be sure to annoy the conceited pigs. He would then issue on on-line challenge, but he would only accept a challenge from the three sibling pigs.

He would bet each of them that they could not correctly answer three of his questions. If they did get all three right, he would work for them for a week for free. If they missed any one question, they would have to work for him for a week for free. Of course, when they came to his house to work for him, he would grab each pig and eat them.

A week later, Jack had set up his website and a picture of him that showed a large handsome looking male pig. His banner had all sorts of pictures of gold coins, silver coins, jewels, exotic cars, and exotic locations. Right in the middle of the banner was the large words "Jack, King of On-Line Gaming Pigs." To the right side of the page was the picture of a large flashing gold treasure chest. Inside the chest, were the words printed in bright colors: **"I challenge you. I know more than you do about anything. Click on to accept my challenge."**

Upon clicking on the treasure box, the description of the challenge and the rewards were printed. It was stated clearly that the challenger would have the right to select the subject matter. Jack felt that this latter stipulation would ensure that the bait would be taken since each pig would be sure to think that no one could be smarter than they were in their specialized area of expertise. Jayla would no doubt select questions on philosophy while Paul would select questions on world literature and Joanne would select questions on physics.

Joanne was the first one of the three pigs to notice the online challenge. "What", she thought, "Who is this arrogant joker that thinks he is so smart? I will show him." She sent back a message which said, "I accept your challenge. The subject is physics. Send me your questions."

Jack sent the following questions. Each question had to be difficult so as not to arouse suspicion but not too difficult. At least, until the third question.

First Question: Do heavier objects fall more slowly than lighter objects?"

Joanne's Answer: No. If an object is heavier the force of gravity is greater, but since it has greater mass the acceleration is the same, so it moves at the same speed.

Second Question: What is the difference between energy and power?

Joanne's Answer: Power is the rate of energy being generated or consumed.

"Yes," wrote Jack "You have been correct on the first two questions." Now thought Jack, I will give her the most difficult and impossible question to answer since my thought question is a paradox.

Third Question: We place a living cat into a steel chamber, along with a device containing a vial of hydrocyanic acid. There is, in the chamber, a small amount of hydrocyanic acid, a radioactive substance. If even a single atom of the substance decays during the test period, a relay mechanism will trip a hammer, which will, in turn, break the vial and kill the cat. Is the cat dead or alive?

Joanne's Answer: That's not fair because it is a paradoxical question. According to quantum theory, the cat is both alive and dead until I open the box and look. You cannot know which state the cat is in without opening the box.

Jack's reply, "However, you agreed to the questions and now you must work for me for a week."

Well, Joanne thought, he's not such a bad looking pig so maybe it will be fun.

She went to the address that Jack gave and knocked on the door. Just as soon as Jack opened the door he pounced on poor Joanne and in a few bites entirely gobbled her up.

Next to reply to Jack's challenge was Paul. Jack had changed the picture on his web site and now presented himself as a young extremely attractive looking female pig. He changed his internet name to Jacqueline. Paul saw the picture and even without the challenge was rather intrigued by the picture of Jacqueline. Paul replied to Jacqueline's challenge and requested world literature as the subject for his three questions.

First Question: Who wrote the book, <u>The Importance of Living</u>?

Paul's Answer: That's easy. It was Lin Yutang

Second Question: How many lines does a Shakespearean sonnet have?

Paul's Answer: Another easy one. It has 14 lines.

Now thought Jack for the paradox question. Paul thinks he is so smart. I can hardly wait to have more roast pork for dinner.

Third Question: This sentence is not a paradox. – True or false

Paul's Answer: There is no way I can answer that question. First, the sentence cannot be false. If it were false, then it would not be a paradox, since any sentence that is a paradox must be true. But it says that it is not a paradox, so this would mean that what it says is the case, and hence it would be true. This is a contradiction.

Jack's reply, "Sorry, you played the game, and you could not answer all three questions. So you lost. When do you want to come over to my house and start working?

Paul thought Jacqueline looked pretty cute and would like to meet her anyway and so he replied, "How about I come over to your place tonight and we have dinner together?"

Jack answered, "Great, I love the idea. I will make a wonderful meal for us together."

That was the last that anyone saw of Jack the pig with a Ph.D. in World Literature.

Two more weeks went by and Jack changed his website back to a picture with a handsome young male pig with his own name of Jack. He felt sure that with the challenge and the picture of a good-looking pig, he would soon entice Jayla to take up the challenge.

Now Jayla had not seen her siblings for the past four weeks. She knew that they loved to play on-line games and she had not seen them around any of the usual game sites. She surfed the web each day but could not find any games they were playing. It appeared that the last game any of them played was at the site of some arrogant guy who billed himself as the King of On-line Gaming Pigs. Her web skills showed her that both of her siblings had accepted his challenge. She pondered the coincidence that since accepting the challenge, she had not seen either sibling again. This raised some suspicions in her mind. Nevertheless, she decided to accept the challenge but with a bit of caution. She posted her acceptance on the website and stated her chosen subject field as philosophy.

Jack was overjoyed. He loved roast pig and was ready for his third pig of the year. He would be cautious and not try to tip his hand, so he researched the three questions very carefully. He was quite sure that the third one would be unanswerable.

First Question: Do states have moral authority over their citizens?

Jayla's Answer: Only over those citizens who make an uncoerced decision to give that authority to their state, which I think is almost never.

Jack Replies: Ok, I will concede that one to you.

Second Question: Plato's definition of knowledge was?

Jayla's Answer: Justified true belief.

Jayla had gotten the first two right, but Jack was now ready to spring the paradoxical question on her. There was no way she could get the right answer.

Suddenly, Jack noticed a text that appeared on his computer screen. Jayla was requesting a short break before the next question. Jack could not believe his eyes. Jayla suggested that Jack come over to her house tomorrow night for dinner and bring the third question with him. This was too good to be true. He would get a free dinner before he ate his third pig. He agreed and Jayla texted him her home address.

Now, if you know anything about philosophy, you know that it means the love of wisdom. Jayla was the wisest of the three pigs and she had prepared for the unexpected. Jack the wolf came dressed up in a pig disguise, but Jayla saw right through it. She was not entirely surprised since she had long suspected some treachery was involved. She invited Jack in.

"Jack," said Jayla, "can I give you a drink before dinner?"

"Sure" replied Jack. Jack thought he might as well have a drink before he ate Jayla.

Jayla, knowing full well that Jack was a wolf disguised as a pig prepared him a special martini mixed with some potent knock out drops. Jack would not know what hit him.

Jack took the drink thinking all the time that this was too good to be true. The next thing Jack knew he was waking up with a splitting headache. As he tried to move his muscles, he found that he was tied by all four legs to a sturdy oak chair. Jayla stood over him with a baseball bat.

Reader, let us pause a minute here.

We have now come to a tricky point in our story. We have two dilemmas to solve before we can reach a conclusion. The first problem is how do we bring Jayla's two siblings back? We know the wolf ate both but that is beside the point. We can't have a fairy tale where two siblings get eaten and do not return. It's just not done.

The second problem is what do we do with the big bad wolf? Do we kill him, let him go, castrate him or what? We need to have some type of fitting denouement for Jack the wolf. Again, since this is a fairy tale, we probably need to rule out killing him or castration, but I don't think we can just let him go. Not much drama in that anyway. Let's tackle first problems first.

We will start with getting Jayla's two siblings back.

Jayla took the bat and whacked the big bad wolf right in the stomach. Lo and behold, the wolf gave a big burp and out popped Paul. One more smack to the stomach and out popped Joanne. The siblings were all so happy to see each other and Jayla that they hugged and hugged for a mighty long time.

Ok, so they were eaten. It's a fairy tale and we can do anything as implausible as we desire. After all, you did not complain when a wolf ate a 400-pound pig, so don't start nitpicking now.

Once pleasantries were over, the three pigs sat down to discuss the fate of Jack the big bad wolf. Paul wanted to cut him into many pieces and scatter him all over the neighborhood. Joanne wanted to skin him alive and use his fur for a rug. Jayla cautioned restraint. "Remember," she said, "this is a fairy tale, and we can't do such gruesome things to the big bad wolf in a fairy tale." Jayla suggested that they all do an internet search and see what kinds of options for dealing with pig eating wolfs they might find. They would each Google some strategies and then discuss ideas.

A few hours went by and both Paul and Joanne each came up with an idea. Jayla was still undecided and had not found any ideas that really thrilled her. Paul suggested that they put Jack in a box and ship him to Antarctica. Joanne thought that maybe through behavioral modification they could convince Jack that he did not want to eat pigs. Jayla thought both ideas were not a fitting end to a good fairy tale. She then had a brainstorm. Let's have a contest!

Here is Jayla's idea for the contest. Our readers will help us to find a fitting conclusion to this story. Everyone who reads this story is invited to suggest a conclusion. Take a few minutes to think of what the three pigs can do with the big bad wolf so that they will have a fitting end to this tale. Send us your ideas via email. The three "not so little" pigs will select their favorite reader suggested idea.

We all look forward to getting your solutions as to what they should do with Jack, the big bad wolf. **They cannot keep him tied up forever**. Send your ideas to 3pigs@notsolittle.com

Time for Questions:

What will we do with the big bad wolf? Do you remember how this story ended in the original version? Do you like fairy tales? Why or why not? What is the point of a fairy tale? Is there a point to this story? What is it?

Alexa, I Need a Date for Saturday Night!

Introduction

Alexa has become ubiquitous in our lives. Each day we buy more Alexa apps and each day the apps get smarter and smarter. I hesitate to tell you how often my wife and I use Alexa each day. I can only ponder how we lived without her. I thought the following story might be another use for Alexa. If only I were single again!

Alexa, I Need a Date for Saturday Night!

Friday Morning

John: Alexa. Can you find me a date for Saturday night?

Alexa: Which sexual persuasion do you prefer, gay, lesbian, bisexual, transsexual, transgender, or straight?

John: I would like straight.

Alexa: Do you prefer male or female?

John: Female.

Alexa: What age range do you prefer: 20-25, 25-30, 30-40, 40-50, 50-60, 60 and over?

John: 20-25 please.

Alexa: What body shape do you like: thin, voluptuous, statuesque, petite, pudgy, full bodied or rotund?

John: I prefer voluptuous.

Alexa: Are you looking for a long-term partner or a simple hook-up?

John: A simple hook-up.

Alexa: How far are you willing to travel for this date, 10-20 miles, 20-50 miles, over 50 miles?

John: I prefer 10-20 miles.

Alexa: Searching…Searching.

Alexa: I believe I have a hit. Mary (no last name given) is also searching for a date for Saturday night with male characteristics that are similar to those you have input. I will check for receptivity on her part.

A few minutes later

Alexa: Mary has some questions for you, John.

John: Alexa, what are her questions?

Alexa: What kind of movies do you like?

John: Action adventure.

Alexa: What is your favorite place to eat in Casa Grande?

John: I like the Olive Garden and Mimi's.

Alexa: What are your favorite hobbies?

John: I like traveling, music, reading and jogging.

Alexa: I will check back with Mary.

A few minutes later

Alexa: Mary has agreed to a date. She would like to go to dinner with you at the Olive Garden and then a movie.

John: How will I recognize her?

Alexa: Checking…Checking.

Alexa: Mary will be wearing a bright red dress and a red scarf.

John: That will work Alexa, I will find her.

Sunday Morning

John: Alexa!

Alexa: What is it, John?

John: I had a horrible date on Saturday night.

Alexa: What went wrong John?

John: Mary was nothing like I asked for. She was overweight, about 50 years old and looking for a long-term relationship. She was far from voluptuous.

Alexa: Feedback from Mary was similar to yours John.

John: Alexa! Please explain.

Alexa: Mary reported back that you were skinny and not muscular. You were closer to 70 than 40,. You were bald, and you did not have a large yacht in the Caribbean.

John: Well, I might have exaggerated a little on my characteristics.

John: Alexa! Let's try again for this Saturday night.

Alexa: Please input requirements John.

John: I want a 25-year-old voluptuous blond who would like a simple hookup with an overweight, bald, 70-year-old man with no money.

Alexa: Searching…Searching.

Several Hours Later

John: Alexa! Have you found a woman like I described yet?

Alexa: I have searched all of the United States, all five continents as well as the entire Universe, no results found for such a woman as you describe.

John: Alexa! Where is the best place to get a pizza in Casa Grande for Saturday night?

Alexa: According to Yelp, the best pizza is at Papa Murphy's on Florence Street in Casa Grande. They have a 4.2-star rating based on thirty reviewers. Should I order you a pizza for Saturday night?

Time for Questions:

Do you own an Alexa device? Are you planning to purchase one? Why or why not? Have you experienced what such devices can do? What do you think will come next?

Tommy, A Boy for All Seasons

Introduction

This is a story about my best friend in high school. His name was Thomas Donnelly. This story takes place over fifty years ago. I still think of the influence that these events have had on my life. Some of you will be repelled by the story that I narrate. If you can suspend your morality, you might be able to accept that the culture I grew up in made these events normal even if you do not consider them to be moral.

Tommy, A Boy for All Seasons

It happened one hot Saturday afternoon in the summer. I was hanging out on our Manton Street corner. As with all Italian male teenagers, we hung out in a certain geographic area and this association led to our identity as the "Manton Gang." Manton was a suburb of Providence R.I. and a primarily Italian neighborhood. My father was Italian, and my mother was Irish. It was just the reverse for my best friend Tommy. His mother was Italian, and his father was Irish. Nevertheless, anyone with Irish or Italian blood was accepted into our street corner gang.

From fourteen to eighteen years of age, few of us were interested in anything except gambling and sex. Gambling tended to be a regular event on the corner where we hung out, but sex was much more episodic. Good Italian girls in the sixties still did not have sex outside of marriage. This left us to find those "bad girls" whose discrimination did not tend towards marriage or even long-term love affairs. They were less choosy in terms of selecting "affairs of the heart."

Tommy and I were sitting on the corner discussing nothing important when a blue and white 56 Ford four door Fairlane pulled up to the curb and started honking. At first, we did not recognize anyone in the car. Two guys were in the front seat and no one was in the back seat. We finally recognized Dave and Bob. Dave was an infrequent corner member, but Bob was a regular. We sauntered over to the car. It was always important to look cool and nonchalant when we were growing up. As we approached the open window on Dave's side, he yelled out. "Hey, you guys want to get laid?"

"What's up?" I asked. Dave replied, "Get in and I will tell you on the way." Both Tommy and I jumped in the back seat. Bob already had shot gun. Dave gunned the accelerator and off we went. "Okay, so where are we going?" asked Tommy. Bob answered, "There is this chick, and she is hot to go with anyone who comes over to her house." "You mean she will take all of us? What's wrong with her?" I wanted to know. Bob continued, "Who knows. She is just really open to more than one guy." "Where are her parents?" I persisted. "She lives with her dad who is a police chief," said Dave. "What, are you crazy?" both Tommy and I asked in synchrony. "Don't worry," assured Bob, "Her dad will not be home."

The idea of sex in our minds easily overrode any caution or concern about getting caught by her father. We arrived at her house. She lived out of town near Scituate which is a more rural area of Rhode Island in the sixties. When we arrived, Bob said, "I will go in first and check things out. If it is okay, you guys can come in." Bob went inside the small average looking New England Colonial house with two upper dormer windows and came out a few minutes later. "OK, guys." Bob said, "She is willing." We all trotted inside the house to the first room which was a kitchen with a small table and four chairs. Dave, Tommy, and I sat on the chairs and Bob headed up a small staircase. "I will go first," said Bob "and Dave is next. You and Tommy can decide who goes after Dave." "Oh," remembered Bob, "her name is Barbara, and she likes to be called Barb." No one challenged this order of affairs as it was taken for granted that since Bob had set this up, he had first dibs.

Bob marched up the stairs while Dave, Tommy and I just sat and kibitzed. I wondered what was in store for me when I went up the stairs. Bob came down about twenty minutes later looking quite proud and content. "She likes to talk a little before," explained Bob, "so you have to be a little patient. But be persistent and she will get on with it."   It was Dave's turn next and he wasted no time going up the staircase. Sometime later Dave came down, also looking proud and content.

Tommy and I decided that I would go next. Up the staircase I went and into a small bedroom where I found Barb half-dressed and sitting on the edge of the bed. She was an extremely attractive young girl of sixteen or seventeen years of age. She had long brown hair and a small frame that was nicely curved. She had a pretty face and could easily have been a cheerleader. She was probably about five feet four inches in height, but it was somewhat difficult to tell as she was sitting cross legged on her bed.

I introduced myself. We started some small talk and I learned that her mother had left her father some time ago and that she now lived alone with her dad. She had no other siblings. Her dad was strict and would not let her date. She said that he scared most of her friends away and was difficult to live with. I sensed that her escapades today were a chance for her to rebel against her father's strict sexual codes. She was willing to go all out and did not care about any side effects. No birth control or sexual disease prevention even came up as a precaution.

We talked for about a half hour or so and I sensed that I had better get on with the action or she would talk forever. A real man talks less than he acts, and I had talked longer than most real men would have. I started to lay Barbara down on the bed. She put up no resistance and meekly laid back against the sheets. I placed my body down over hers but before starting to remove any of our clothes, I gazed into her eyes. They were brown and sad. I stopped to think. This poor girl is looking for someone to love her and does not really know how to go about it. I would just be taking advantageous of her. I can't do this. I lifted her back up and quietly left the room. She never said a word to me, and I left without speaking another word.

Feeling very guilty, I walked back down the staircase. Dave and Bob were gone. I glanced outside. They had gone back to the car and were now playing cards in the front seat. Hi Low Jack, was a popular game on the corner and we played it for money whatever chance we had. I returned to the kitchen and said to Tommy, "It's your turn." Tommy went up the staircase and returned about thirty minutes later. We silently left the house by the front door. I never saw Barb or that house again.

We piled back in the car with Dave and Bob. There was some minor discussion about Barbara and how hot she was that took place between Dave and Bob. Neither Tommy nor I said I word. Truth be told, I would never have admitted to either Dave or Bob that I did not have sex with Barb. Tommy and I were dropped back at the Manton Street corner. Dave and Bob drove off together.

Tommy and I sat quietly for a while on the curb. I finally broke the silence and asked Tommy, "How did it go?" Tommy looked pensive and replied, "I did not do a thing with Barb except to talk to her." I was somewhat stunned as I figured that I had wimped out but that Tommy (who was one of the best-looking guys on the corner) would have scored a home run in sixty seconds flat. I asked Tommy, "Why?" I did not tell him that I had also struck out. At the time, that is how I felt: like a batter who comes up to the plate, takes three swings and strikes out.

Tommy quietly replied "I did not want to take advantage of her. She was lonely and scared and needy. She needed a friend more than she needed to get laid." I had felt the same way but many years ago, pride and ego would not allow me to admit that I had also not gone all the way with Barb. I persisted, "What are you going to tell the other guys?" Tommy then replied with a statement that I have remembered for the rest of my life. **"I don't care what they think, I have to live with myself."**

Over the years, I had lost touch with Tommy. I eventually found his phone number and called him. We had traveled quite different roads. Tommy became a minister and works with the poor. I became an educator and management consultant. Many years and many different philosophies now separate us. However, I will never forget the lesson that I learned from Tommy that one hot summer afternoon about integrity and being who we are called to be and not who the world wants us to be.

Time for Questions:

Why do I call Tommy a "boy for all seasons?" What does it mean to have integrity? How do we develop integrity? How do we increase our empathy for other people? What does it mean "to be ourselves"? Are people naturally good or evil?

Samson and Delilah: A Modern Fable

Introduction

This is my version of the story of Samson and Delilah. It is a story of passion, romance, jealousy, intrigue, narcissism and maybe even murder. The setting takes place in Brooklyn, New York. I grew up in Brooklyn and lived there until my parents moved to Rhode Island when I was ten years old. The date for this story is sometime in the 21st Century. It has been many years since I was back to my old neighborhood. This story reflects on some of the ideas I learned about life after leaving New York.

Samson and Delilah: A Modern Fable

Samson was the strongest most well-built man on the block. He had muscles chiseled in stone. His muscles had muscles. He stood 6 feet 4 inches tall and did not have an ounce of fat on him.   Samson worked out seven days a week, twice each day at the Philistine Gym on Gideon Street. He worked out before he went to work each morning and after work for two hours each evening.

Samson was easily the most powerful man in the gym. Everybody admired Samson, but not quite as much as Samson admired himself. It was said that he could not pass a mirror without flexing his muscles and taking a few moments to pose in various bodybuilding stances.

Delilah lived in the same neighborhood as Samson. All of her neighbors agreed that she was the most beautiful woman they had ever seen. She was tall with long blond hair and a perfectly proportioned figure. Men could not help stopping in their tracks to stare when she walked by. She looked like an angel. She was so beautiful that many local artists would try to paint her from memory.

Delilah also went to the same gym as Samson. All the guys in the gym would flex their biceps or triceps an extra amount each time that Delilah came near them. All except Samson. He seldom even noticed Delilah. Delilah knew the effect that she had on men, but she could care less. The only man that she was interested in was Samson. Perhaps it was the old story about wanting something more because you can't have it. Delilah had only one other person she admired, herself. Much like Samson, she could not pass by a mirror without staring at her reflection and thinking "how beautiful I am."

Samson wanted to show the world that he was the strongest man who ever lived. To achieve this goal, he decided to attend the World Weightlifting Championship taking place in Brooklyn. He could already dead lift 1000 pounds and he was determined he would lift 1200 pounds to shatter the then current world record of 1102.3 pounds.

Now Samson was a tad superstitious. Because he was lifting more each year and had never cut his hair, he believed that his strength grew proportionately along with the length of his hair. He had let his hair grow for over ten years and his braid was now down almost to his waist. He was certain that his strength was a result of his long hair.

Delilah grew more and more desperate in her attempts to get Samson to notice her. Finally, she hit on the idea to simply approach Samson and remark on his wonderful hair. So, one day while he was practicing his dead lifts, she sauntered by and casually remarked on how beautiful his hair was. She proceeded to compliment him on his marvelous muscle definition. She followed up these compliments with the suggestion that they go back to her place after working out and she would cook him a nice microwave dinner and brush his hair. This idea delighted Samson and after working out, they both went to Delilah's house.

As you would guess, human nature being what it was, dinner turned into dessert, dessert turned into a night cap, and a night cap woke up with breakfast. After that evening, Delilah and Samson were a twosome. Both loved each other with a passion only matched by their mutual admiration for themselves. It was a question of whom or which they loved more.

As you may know, narcissists have a short attention span for anything but themselves. Samson was the first to break the implicit arrangement that seemed to characterize their relationship. Thus, one evening, Delilah knocked on Samson's door and much to her surprise another woman in a skimpy negligee answered. Delilah was shocked but more than shocked she was furious. She swore revenge on Samson.

Weeks went by, Samson ignored Delilah at the gym and Delilah ignored Samson. However, all this time Delilah was plotting her revenge. She well knew that the big weightlifting event was coming up and she also knew that Samson was superstitious about his hair and strength. This latter fact was the pillar of her idea for revenge.

Delilah waited until the night before the World Weightlifting Championship. At around midnight, she used the key that Samson hid near his door to let herself into Samson's apartment. Moving as stealthily as a cat, she entered Samson's bedroom. Samson was a sound sleeper, and he had no inclination of what awaited him. Delilah took the surgical scalpel that she had borrowed from a medical admirer and in one quick slash, she lopped off Samson's braid. Samson was totally unaware and did not move a muscle. Delilah slipped back out the way she had come and placed Samson's key back where he hid it.

The next morning Samson woke and went to the bathroom to get ready for the big event. Imagine his surprise and chagrin when he looked in the mirror and found that most of his hair was gone. Samson was devastated. He immediately knew that Delilah had taken her revenge. There was no way that he could dead lift without his hair. His thoughts ran to the best way to get even with Delilah and whether or not her murder would constitute justifiable homicide.

Samson decided to go to the championship event anyway. Perhaps, even without his long hair, he would still have a chance. Sadly, he could not even dead lift 800 pounds. This was the minimum weight needed to qualify for the competitive championship rounds. The mighty Samson was only a shell of his old self. Everyone who knew him wondered what had happened to the once proud and haughty Samson. Was this God's way of punishing the narcissistic among us?

History shows that Samson never broke another record, and his name was gradually erased from the rolls of major body builders and weightlifters at the Philistine Gym.

What of Delilah? Would you like to know how she got her just rewards? You see every moral or fable must have a denouement. The good guy triumphs over the bad guy. The two lovers marry and live happily ever after. The struggling athlete scores the final points to win the big game. The starving painter is eventually recognized for her creative genius. The hero slays the dragon and wins the fair maid.

Unfortunately, neither Delilah's neighbors nor the historians at the Philistine Gym have any further records for Delilah. It is like she vanished into thin air immediately after the big weightlifting event. There are those who suspect that foul play may have played a role in her mysterious departure. Others say she got put on weight, lost her looks, married a computer geek and is living in Poughkeepsie.

Time for Questions:

What was the source of Samson's power? Was it really his hair? What makes anyone powerful? What role does belief have in our powers? Can you really accomplish anything without believing in yourself? What happens when you stop believing in yourself?

Irony, Paradox, and Serendipity or Why a Donkey Knew Best!

Introduction

A good friend of mine is from Nigeria. He is a forensics computer expert and is wise in the ways of the world. His name is Israel and I always love talking to him. My idea for this story came from a story that he told me some time ago. He said that it was an old African folk tale. I have adapted the story and Israel might have a hard time recognizing it now. A writer always likes to embellish a little. In this case, I may have embellished a great deal.

Irony, Paradox, and Serendipity or Why a Donkey Knew Best!

Once upon a time, back when animals could talk and people did not rule the world, there was a donkey named Isaiah. Isaiah was the wisest animal in the land. He knew everything about life and death. All of the animals, even the owls, came to Isaiah when they had a question they could not answer or when they had a key decision to make. The most intelligent people in the world would also come to Isaiah when they had a problem they could not solve. Isaiah was not only intelligent, but he was kind as well. Now that might seem like a paradox to some. Can we be intelligent and also kind?

Were not the managers at Enron Corporation the "smartest men in the room?" Maybe, but Enron's greedy senior management would hardly seem to qualify as kindhearted when you consider the damage they did to the lives of their employees. In truth, it often seems that the greatest paradoxes of all time, involve the harm done by "highly intelligent people." The world is full of examples of smart people who do great harm because they care little for the feelings or welfare of others.

Fortunately for the world, Isaiah was not this kind of creature. He was the epitome of wisdom because he combined intelligence with feelings and empathy for others.

No matter what the problem, Isaiah would always consider the potential damage and impact on others of his decisions and choices. Whenever he reasoned out a problem, the morals and ethics of the problem were just as important to Isaiah as the solutions. Causing damage to anyone was not seen as a good solution. Some of the people and animals were skeptical that Isaiah could always find a win-win solution but somehow Isaiah always did. Many people often find that the key decisions they make result in ironic outcomes that they would not have been able to predict. This was not the case with Isaiah's solutions. His outcomes were never ironic. Isaiah seemed to have the ability (like Merlin the Wizard) to foresee the future. Within the unlimited possibilities of various timelines that the future laid out, Isaiah could always find the optimal path.

Once when one of the animals asked Isaiah how he managed to construct such robust solutions, he attributed his ability to serendipity. According to Isaiah, his ideas were often happy accidents which surprised him with their elegance and simplicity. How could serendipity be the answer when he was always 100 accurate. Thus, another paradox, how could serendipitous decision-making result in outcomes that are always beneficial? Luck may favor the prepared mind but even luck has its limits. Isaiah's abilities seemed to be more of a miraculous nature than of a serendipitous nature. If so, this is truly ironic since Isaiah did not believe in miracles.

However, as with all good things, they must eventually come to an end. Isaiah grew old in years and tired in body if not sometimes in spirit. He had less energy for solving the problems of the world and gradually the animals and humans stopped coming to him for solutions. The various species retreated further and further from each other. Humans built houses and walls and fences to keep themselves in and animals out. The further they distanced from each other, the more they mistrusted each other. Mistrust led do fear. The once harmonious relationship that existed between animals and humans dissolved in a mist of animosity and cruelty.

Animals and humans started killing and eating former friends. Excuses for killing became the norm and humans declared a theory called "Survival of the Fittest." Within this theory, might became right, power dictated the rules and the "fittest" could dominate those deemed as less fit. Whole species were seen as suitable for consumption by other species. Every species was a commodity. Any species with no commercial value went to the bottom of the economic pile.

People started schools and a theory of Human Resources became the norm in colleges. Business Majors, Legal Majors and Medical Majors are paid more than English Majors, History Majors, Art Majors and Philosophy Majors. College students are paid more than high school students. Those who were loyal to the economic engines of society are given high status and high paying jobs.

Sadly, Isaiah saw all this but could find no solutions to the problems or trends. Eventually, though he lived for many hundreds of years, people just regarded him as that "dumb old donkey" who did not say much. As time passed, most people and animals even forgot that Isaiah had a brain or could speak. Isaiah did not feel the need to disabuse anyone of their conceptions and so he just kept to himself. At the age of 5887 years Isaiah died. His body was sent to a glue factory to be processed. He left no legacy of writings, nor any erudite body of knowledge, nor any great poetry, nor any glorious music. He was remembered as just another old donkey that brayed and died.

Some if they had known Isaiah. might have chided him for not posting his ideas and thoughts on Facebook or YouTube. At least that way, he might have achieved some measure of fame if not fortune. Ironically, or paradoxically, or serendipitously, (choose one), it never occurred to Isaiah to become either Internet or Google savvy or famous or rich. History may someday rediscover his genius and perhaps he will yet be remembered in homage for his major contributions to world peace for thousands of years.

By the way, it is generally believed or was at least "once upon a time" that Isaiah (and not Euripides or Aeschylus or Sophocles) was the author of <u>Irony</u>, <u>Paradox</u> and <u>Serendipity.</u> These three concepts were widely used by Isaiah in his conversations and discussions with humans and animals. Thus, while the three words today bear an etymology that derives from Greek vocabulary, their usage in practice and ideology must be attributed to Isaiah, the Donkey.

Time for Questions:

Can you give me an example of irony or serendipity or paradox in your life? What do ideas matter anyway or do they not? What if everyone was a philosophy major? What would happen if more people practiced kindness instead of hate? What value do animals have? Are they just commodities? What if we were all vegetarians? Would it make any difference to the world?

Buddha and the Duck

Introduction

This is my contribution to the life of Buddha. There have been many prophets, but few are as amazing as the Buddha. Years ago, I was involved in a Zen Monastery where I went to meditate each week. I read a great deal of literature on Zen Buddhism but until recently never thought of writing a story about Buddha. Many people have written stories about his life. I hope mine will inspire you to study his philosophy more.

Buddha and the Duck

My birth name is Siddhartha Gautama. I became known as Buddha. I was born into a rich family. I was living a life of privilege with servants and maids to cater to my every whim. I had no need to work to earn money since my family had more gold than we knew what to do with. My days were full of eating, drinking, playing, and indulging my whims. As I grew older, I could see that my life was going nowhere. It had no meaning or purpose beyond my daily pleasures. I soon decided that I must leave my palace to find out what life was really about. I left home when I turned twenty. My goal was to find the true meaning and purpose of my life.

It was a sweltering day in July, and I was trudging down yet another long dusty road somewhere between China and India. I had been walking these unnamed roads for many months now. The only meaning I was finding was the dust and sweat covering my skin from my exertions on these unpaved rural paths. I was becoming more and more depressed as my journey now seemed fruitless. I was about to conclude that life was hopeless and that I would never find my true meaning and purpose.

As I walked over a rise in the road, I saw a duck waddling across the road. I called out in jest "Hey, Mr. Duck why are you crossing the road?" I started to laugh when all of a sudden, I thought I heard the duck say, "Why do you think stupid?" Clearly taken aback, I looked around to see where the voice had come from. "What are you looking for dummy?" This time I was sure that the duck was talking, and it was looking directly at me. I began to think that the summer sun was addling my brain. I spoke loudly, "Ducks cannot talk. You are an illusion." "Well, now" said the duck, "another human who thinks they know everything."

"Okay, just supposing that you really are able to talk, why are you talking to me?" "You asked me your dumb question, so I thought that I would reply to you. Most of the time, it is not worth bothering conversing with humans since their only thoughts are about sex, food, drink and money."

"I am not like everyone else. I am traveling in search of the meaning and purpose of life and particularly my own life. I do not care about sex, food, drink or money."

"Ha!" mocked the duck. "You think that you are so special that you have a meaning or purpose ordained by the gods for your existence."

"You raise an interesting point, Mr. Duck. I simply assumed that we all had a purpose for existence."

"You humans are always assuming things. You think that the world and everything in it are made for your purposes. You believe that you are the center of the universe and everything revolves around you."

"I think instead of crossing this road, I will also journey down the road and look for the meaning and purpose of my life," chortled the duck with a funny cackling laugh.

"You are making fun of me," I protested.

"Why is it funny to think of ducks looking for the purpose and meaning of their lives? Should it be any funnier than humans looking for their purpose and meaning?"

"You humans are all the same," continued the duck, "You think that you are so important."

"But what," I asked, "If there is no purpose or meaning to anyone's life?"

"There would be no worry, no power trips, no greed, no lust, no hate, no war," answered the duck.

"Are you saying that all of the problems humans have come from a search for meaning and purpose?"

"I am not saying anything." the duck responded. "I am only walking to the other side of the road. Then, I will be on my way again. I hope you have a good day."

"Good day to you as well, Mr. Duck."

The duck continued on his way across the road and through the brush until he was no longer visible to me. His last question had left me in a quandary. What if all of my discomfort and unhappiness came because I was searching for meaning and purpose? What if these were truly irrelevant concepts to the universe? What if I stopped this search and could simply BE as the duck was? Eat when I am hungry. Sleep when I am tired. Walk when I feel like it.

Free the mind from disturbances. Get rid of entanglements. Simply BE.

"Teach this triple truth to all: A generous heart, kind speech, and a life of service and compassion are the things which renew humanity." — Buddha

"Life has no meaning. Each of us has meaning and we bring it to life. It is a waste to be asking the question when you are the answer." — Joseph Campbell

Muhammad and the Christian Money Lender

Introduction

I wrote this story as part of my series on the great prophets. I believe every religion in the world has something to offer. I also believe that too many religions preach as though theirs was the "one true religion" and all others are inferior. I grew up Roman Catholic but now consider myself somewhere between an atheist and an agnostic. I do not challenge anyone whose faith compels them to believe in a god. There is room in the world for many different viewpoints.

Muhammad and the Christian Money Lender

My name is Muhammad. I was born in 570 CE. My father died the year before I was born. My mother died when I was only six years old. I was raised by a succession of family members until I was a young man. I was then sent to live with my uncle Abu Talib. My uncle was a merchant, and it was hoped that I could learn a commercial trade from him. We traveled far and wide over many of the trading routes between the Indian Ocean and the Mediterranean Sea. He taught me how to be an honest trader. When I was eighteen, I decided that I had learned enough from my uncle and that it was time to go out on my own. This story is about how I became an independent merchant.

It was a beautiful sunny morning in early March. I had decided to walk to the marketplace in Jeddah near where I was staying to see what wares and goods were for sale. It had become my intention to buy and sell rugs. I loved the beauty and craftsmanship that went into an Arabian rug. I could always feel proud that these were my products and that I was making the world a more beautiful place by sharing these fine Arabian rugs with others. I never lied to my clients and I never made false or exaggerated claims to any people. I was given the nickname "al-Amin" meaning faithful or trustworthy.

I was walking around the marketplace perusing the various wares of the other merchants. In one of the alley ways I noticed a booth with a sign that read: "المال للإقراض" or "Money for Lending." Suddenly, I had an idea. If I could borrow some money, I could afford to buy a few more rugs. Typically, I was short of money to buy enough rugs. It would be much more worthwhile going on a caravan with enough rugs for my potential buyers.

I walked up to the booth and greeted the merchant. "Ahlan wa Sahlan." He replied: "Ahlan wa Sahlan; my name is Musa. I am a Christian money lender, and I am happy to make your acquaintance. How can I help you?"

I thought about his question for a brief second. "I would like to borrow money to help finance my rug business. I can only afford a few rugs now but if I had more money, I could buy extra rugs."

The money lender looked at me carefully and then answered: "It will take two things before I can give you some money. The first is the collateral for the money that you need."

"I am not familiar with the term collateral Sir," I responded. "What is collateral?"

"It is something that you give me so that if you fail to pay me back the money that I lend you, I will be able to sell your collateral and recover my money. It might be some jewelry or gold or rugs that you will provide me to keep until you repay me."

"Mr. Musa, I do not have any collateral that I can give you. I only have my good name. I am known far and wide as an honest merchant who never cheats anyone. I always ask a fair price for my goods. People call me 'al Amin' because I always pay my debts and I am very trustworthy."

"Hmm," said Mr. Musa. "I guess I can ignore the first requirement for my money since you have such a good honest reputation. Now all we need to agree on is the interest that you will pay me for the loan. Would you agree to pay me back at five percent per month of the total amount that I lend you?

"Mr. Musa, I do not understand this idea of interest. What is the interest for?"

"It is my profit or commission for helping you with my money."

"Sir, did you not say that you are a Christian and are not Christians followers of the prophet Jesus Christ?"

"Yes, young man, I am a Christian and I am a believer in Jesus. But what does Jesus have to do with us doing business?"

"Sir, I thought Jesus taught his followers to help the poor and needy. Did he not say, **'Give to everyone who asks you, and if anyone takes what belongs to you, do not demand it back?'** Then why Mr. Musa would you want to take money from me for helping me?"

"Young man, you do not understand the ways of the world. Many things are spoken by the prophets, but one does not always live by their words. In a perfect world, I suppose one could follow the path trod by Jesus, but Jesus did not live in our times. If you do not feel that my terms are fair, then you do not have to borrow my money.

"Mr. Musa, I am disappointed in the Christianity that you claim. I think that this idea of interest is unneighborly and even seems to me to be greedy. I think a religion should not allow such greed to exist. If I were establishing a religion, I would make it a sin to charge interest to help others."

"O ye who believe! Devour not usury, doubling and quadrupling (the sum lent). Observe your duty to Allah, that ye may be successful." — Qur'an **(3:130)**

Muhammad went on his way and left the merchant looking puzzled and scratching his head. "There goes a man who will never amount to anything" thought Mr. Musa.

"The invention of money opened a new field to human avarice by giving rise to usury and the practice of lending money at interest while the owner passes a life of idleness." — Pliny the Elder

"It is easier for a camel to pass through the eye of a needle than for a rich man to enter the kingdom of God." — Mark (10:25)

A Simple Man Meets Faust

Introduction

In this world of juxtaposition and dialectical opposites, there does not seem to be any two individuals who could be further apart than Ricky Van Shelton's "Simple Man," and Johan Wolfgang von Goethe's "Faust." However, looks and paradigms can often be deceiving. I wrote this piece to compare and contrast the similarities and differences between what on the surface might seem like two quite different people.

A Simple Man Meets Faust

A Simple Man (since we don't know his actual name he will remain a "Simple Man") is a good old country boy. We presume he is a blue-collar worker, never went to college and probably does some hard manual labor. He loves to hunt, fish and drink with Bubba, Billy Joe, and the other boys. He is everyman's down to earth guy. He does not worry about the future but takes life one day at a time. His thoughts are more likely to center around finding his next fishing hole than to try and plumb the meaning of the universe.

Faust for all apparent purposes has not a thing in common with the Simple Man. Faust is complex, morose, introverted, elderly and a true intellectual. Faust went to Leipzig University and the University of Stroudsburg. Both high class German schools. He ranked not only first in his class but first in every academic endeavor he ever undertook. He went on to become the most esteemed Doctor of Philosophy in German and European history. He loved to read, write, compose, and publish esoteric treatises on the nature of the universe and the meaning of reality. Faust is ranked first among the many thinkers and intellectuals in history.

Well, there you have it. Two diametrically opposed male personalities. A Simple Man and his apparently mirror image Faust. But beware! Appearances can be deceiving. Things may not always be as they seem. Could it be that Faust and a Simple Man have more in common than you would think? Follow me as we regard a dialogue between a Simple Man and his wife and a dialogue between Faust and Mephistopheles, the devil. Note similarities. Note differences. A Simple Man wants to find peace of mind and it appears that the woman he calls his "baby" does not understand his real needs.

Faust is distraught and agitated. Despite Faust's soaring intellect, he is unhappy with his life and the success he has achieved. Mephistopheles appears to him and offers him a deal for his soul. Mephistopheles purports to be able to give Faust the happiness he desires.

The dialogue for A Simple Man and Faust are taken from the following sources:

- "I Am a Simple Man," (Lyrics by Walt Aldridge and Recorded Music by Ricky Van Shelton)

- "Faust," (An opera in five acts by Charles Gounod to a French libretto by Jules Barbier and Michel Carré from Carré's play Faust et Marguerite, in turn loosely based on Johann Wolfgang von Goethe's Faust, Part One."

A Simple Man:

I don't know why you wanna start with me.

I ain't done nothin' far as I can see.

And I'm worn out from working too hard.

Why don't you give me a break?

Faust:

All to know, all in earth and heaven.

No light illumines the visions, ever,

Thronging my brain; no peace is given.

And I linger, thus sad and weary.

Without power to sunder the chain,

Binding my soul to life always dreary.

Nought do I see! Nought do I know.

- **Both Faust and A Simple Man are worn down and worn out. Both are feeling hopeless.**

 A Simple Man:

I know that lately things ain't been so good.

I'll make it up just like I told you I would.

But I'm tired and I wanna sit down,

To ease a sore backache.

Faust:

Again the light of a new day.

O death! when will thy dusky wings,

Above me hover and give me rest?

- **Both men want peace and rest.**

 A Simple Man:

I wanna a job and a piece of land.

Three squares in my frying pan.

Don't seem so hard to me to understand.

Faust:

Cursed be all of man's vile race.

Cursed be the chains which bind him in his place.

Cursed be visions false, deceiving.

Cursed the folly of believing.

Cursed be dreams of love or hate.

Cursed be souls with joy elate.

Cursed be science, prayer, and faith.

Cursed my fate in life and death.

Infernal king, arise!

- **Science, prayer, and faith cannot provide the peace each man requires. Faust has given up on intellectual solutions while a Simple Man still believes in the joys of work, land, and food.**

A Simple Man:

You say you got some things to talk about,

A lot of problems that we need to work out.

But we just end up fighting.

Why don't you give it a rest?

I don't know what else I can say to you.

I'm doing everything I know to do.

And I can't give you anything more,

When I'm giving my best.

Faust:

I sigh for thy kisses,

It's love I demand.

With ardor unwonted

I long now to burn.

I sigh for the rapture,

Of heart and of sense.

- **What both Faust and a Simple Man really want is love.**

A Simple Man:

I wanna place I can lay my head.

Soft woman and a warm bed,

A little time off before I'm dead.

I'm just a simple man.

Faust:

But I implore in vain.

Let me thy hand take and clasp it.

And behold but thy face once again.

Illum'd by that pale light,

From yonder moon that shines

O'er thy beauteous features shedding

Its faint but golden ray.

- **Faust is more eloquent, but a Simple Man goes to the heart of the matter. I just want a soft woman and a warm bed.**

 A Simple Man:

You say you're having trouble figuring me.

I don't believe I'm such a mystery.

Baby what you get is what you see.

I am a simple man.

Faust:

Again the light of a new day.

O death! when will thy dusky wings,

Above me hover and give me rest?

- **The opera and the country song leave the impression that neither Faust nor a Simple Man obtains the life they want to live. Something is out of kilter that cannot be set right. Tragic expectations on the part of both a Simple Man and Faust are never fulfilled in the real world. Neither books nor hunting, nor ideas nor actions enable either man to find what they are looking for.**

A Zen Master happens to be walking by and overhears the laments of both Faust and a Simple Man. He notes the apparent remorse and confusion of their musings. He is struck by their sadness and attempts to offer some wisdom which he feels might be consoling.

Zen Master:

Life cannot be lived through others. The secret of happiness is to let go of your expectations and to realize that happiness is only obtained through inner wisdom and not through external ideas or things or people.

You, Faust, thought that ideas and your intellect could bring you happiness. When this mode failed, you sold your soul to the devil for the immediate pleasures of the world. You failed in both efforts.

You, A Simple Man, thought that you could escape responsibility for your happiness. You thought your wife would provide you the succor and tranquility which your lifestyle necessitated. You thought she would be the warm pillow and soft bed who would take care of your weary bones. You have also failed to find the peace you desired.

Faust: I am half a man!

Simple Man: And I the other half!

Zen Master: Two halves make a whole!

Time for Questions:

What similarities between a Simple Man and Faust did you find? What differences did you find? What if anything surprised you about their thoughts and needs? Do we focus more on the differences between people than the similarities? Would it make a difference in how we view the world if we saw more similarities between people? Do you think you are different from most people or similar? Why? How have your differences and similarities affected your life?

The Window

Introduction

My wife Karen is a nurse. I have joked many times over the years that I married her to help take care of me in my old age. A while ago it occurred to me that I may be the one needing to take care of her. This was a rather shocking thought since I never considered myself the "caregiver" type. I decided to take some classes on caregiving. I have taken several since making this decision and they have profoundly impacted my thinking on aging. This story was motivated in part by my thoughts and reflections on the role of a caregiver and caretaker.

The Window

I'm sitting here looking out the window. It has taken me nearly sixty-five years but now I understand.

I was a young woman of twenty-five when I met Irene. It was my first job out of college. I had just finished my R.N. program at Regina Nursing School. It took me three years going to school days and working part-time evenings to complete my degree. After finishing school, I applied at several nursing homes since I wanted to work with the elderly. In three weeks, I was hired by the River Birch Nursing Home in New Prague, Minnesota.

My first day on the job was the high point and perhaps also the low point of my life. It was the day I met Irene. My supervisor Michelle started my job orientation by introducing me to the staff I would be working with. She then gave me a brief summary of my work duties. She explained that I would be assigned a wing of the nursing home where I would be in charge of a specific number of residents. We were not to call them patients. Each day, my job would be to take care of the residents that I was assigned and to ensure that they received food, care, and compassion.

Michelle then took me around to the twenty or so residents that I would be responsible for. One by one, she gave me a brief bio and medical review for each person. The last one of my charges was Irene. Michelle said she had saved Irene for last because she would be my most difficult resident.

Irene had been taken into the home about two months prior to my arrival. She appeared to have an advanced case of Alzheimer's Disease (which sixty-five years ago was not identified as such.) She had been living with her only daughter for the past five years, but her daughter had died in a car accident and Irene had no other surviving relatives. Her mother, father and two sisters had died many years before her, and no other family members could be located. Social Services selected the River Birch Nursing Home due to its proximity to her previous neighborhood.

Michelle cautioned me that I should not spend too much time with Irene. She did not speak except to demand being taken in her wheelchair to the same window each day. She would sit and look out the window and was not interested in eating, talking, or socializing in any form. Several of the other nurses had tried to form some type of communication with Irene, but all she would ever say was, "Window, window!" Most of the staff decided that she was simply unfriendly and had stopped trying to spend any time with her.

I was young and naïve. I thought I could surely reach out to Irene and form some
type of bridge which would unite us as human beings. Irene would be my
project. We would become friends.

Each day, I made a special point of taking Irene to her large picture window and
stopping by a few times during my shift to simply chat. I would bring her a
cookie in the morning during the coffee break time and one after lunch during
mid-afternoon coffee break. Irene would never take the cookie or even bother to
look at me. She simply stared out the window.

Over time, I began to wonder what she was looking at. After gazing out the
window myself, all I could see was a large grassy field surrounded by numerous
oaks, maples, and birch trees. On any given day, there might be some grackles or
robins walking out in the field but little else to view. It was a pleasant enough
scene of nature but nothing that I thought could keep anyone's attention for more
than a few minutes, never mind several hours of staring out the window.

On the other side of the large sitting room, there was another picture window. I
noticed that it had a pretty view of a large lake and periodically several sail boats
with brightly covered jibs and mains blowing in the wind would be traversing the
lake. I thought that perhaps Irene might like this view better. I walked over to
where she was sitting in her wheelchair and told her I was going to show
her another view that she could look at. I thought she would enjoy the variety and
the change of scenery. As I started to push Irene's wheelchair away from her
chosen window, she became visibly agitated and started pointing and with a raised
voice saying, "Window, window!" I moved her back to the old window and left
her for the day.

Weeks went by and there was never any change in Irene. Then one day, I went over to see how Irene was doing and I brought her a cookie just in case she changed her mind. I never gave up on somehow connecting with Irene and I thought surely the cookie would be my opening to some sort of friendship. Much to my surprise, she took the cookie from my hand and replied, "Thank you. They're coming, they're coming!" I looked out the window but did not see anyone. I asked, "Irene dear, who is coming?" Irene answered, "Why mom, dad, my sisters and daughter." Poor thing I thought, she is delusional.

Next morning, I came to work and started my rounds. I did not see Irene and I wondered where she was. I checked her room. The bed was made and there was no sign of Irene. I went to see my supervisor to ask about Irene. "I am sorry," Michele said, "She passed away last night and was taken to the funeral home. There will be no services for her as she had no surviving relatives." I went home and cried for her passing. I had never understood her or made a connection with her that I thought was the least bit meaningful.

It is sixty-five years later, and I finally understand Irene. I am sitting here looking out a window from a nursing home where I am now a resident. Each day I look out the same window and I see a different event from my life. I have been amazed at the events that I have witnessed. I have seen my mother giving birth to me. I have seen the birth of each of my sisters and brothers. I witnessed my first communion and my first day in school. I watched my wedding and the birth of each of my children. I was at my husband's funeral again.

During the past few months, I have seen all the major events of my life one after the other in perfect chronological order. I am almost at the end of my journey. There is only one final event. The last event will be when they come for

me. They are getting close. My mom, dad, one sister, two brothers and husband
are coming for me. They are coming to take me home. I must keep looking out
the window or I will miss them.

Time for Questions:

How do we deal with the loss of a loved one when they are still alive? What
connections can we possibly make to bridge the sometimes-unbridgeable gaps
that age has a way of creating? What if our loved ones are still with us even when
we may think they are not? How do we have compassion for people who no
longer seem to recognize or care about us?

Perspiration or Inspiration: Which Is More Important to the Writer?

Inspiration or perspiration, perspiration or inspiration, which is more important? Is inspiration the mother of writing while perspiration is the father? There are weeks when I plan to write a blog on a subject that I have been thinking about for many years. Suddenly out of the blue, I get a crazy thought and I feel compelled to write my blog about this sudden flash of inspiration. These insights might come from something I heard, some bit of news, or just an impulse to write about something. Inspiration has provided the content for about 1/3rd of my blogs. For the other 2/3rds of my blogs, the ideas come from perspiration. I read, research, sit, sweat, and write on the subject.

Some writers will tell you that writing is hard work, and that perspiration is THE key element of the writing craft. They will tell you how they get up every morning and sit down in front of the keyboard and start to write. It will not matter what they write as long as they write. They may grind out one or ten pages each day every week. They discipline themselves to do this day after day, week after week and year after year. If you think about it, this will produce a prodigious amount of work.

Think of writing 3 pages a day for 365 days and you have put out about 3 novels. Think of doing this for ten years and you have put out about 30 novels. With good writing and a bit of luck, you just might find one of your works makes the New York Times Best Seller Lists or the Amazon Top Ten or perhaps the Oprah Book Club List. Once you have broken through with your writing, you may be able to reap the benefits of recognition and acclaim. Some writers simply become "one hit wonders" while others capitalize on a "formula" to keep churning out hit after hit.

"There is nothing to writing. All you do is sit down at a typewriter and bleed." — Ernest Hemingway

Stephen King tells the story of how and why he wrote the Bachman books. After achieving much fame and fortune with his suspense novels, he decided to see if he could start over again and achieve popularity and success under a new name. He published four books under a pseudonym as Richard Bachman. The books (which I enjoyed very much) were nowhere near as popular as the King novels. Before he could finish his experiment, he was outed. The books were then re-released as "The Bachman Books" by Steven King and of course, their sales skyrocketed. Perhaps with time, King would have been able to duplicate his former success, or perhaps not. I have read books by many authors which I think should have become best sellers but did not. Hard work and perspiration for an author does not automatically transfer into major book sales.

"If you don't have time to read, you don't have the time (or the tools) to write. Simple as that." — Stephen King

Inspiration will sometimes take a writer where mere perspiration fears to tread. In my weekly writers' group, I sense that many of the members rely a great deal on inspiration for their themes. The idea of perspiration is anathema to some wordsmiths. Why "force" yourself to write if it is not fun or if you do not feel excited about the idea? According to this school of thought, writing should be a pleasure. You do not subscribe to a weekly time frame of when to write or a quantity to write. You simply write when you feel moved by the spirit or impelled to write by the muse of writing. Inspired writing flows more naturally because it seems to come from somewhere other than the brain. Perspiration writing is driven by intellect and discipline. Inspiration writing is driven by the heart and by the soul.

"There is no greater agony than bearing an untold story inside you." — Maya Angelou, <u>I Know Why the Caged Bird Sings</u>

One of the most famous examples of inspiration writing must surely be Lincoln's Gettysburg Address. It was written on the back of an envelope while he was on a train going to the recent battlefield to give a testimonial to the men and women who fought and died there. Two hundred and seventy or so words depending on which of the four versions you read. Computers and exact copies for things were not as prevalent in 1863 as they are now. It has become one of the most famous and well-known pieces of writing in the history of humanity. You never get tired of hearing this speech or reading it because it truly reflects the soul and spirit of this great human being. Full of repetition and redundancy, it nevertheless achieves a magnificence that can only be attributed to the power of inspiration. No Madison Avenue ad men or White House speech reporters had a hand in the words that Lincoln spoke that day. He did it alone. Speech writers today would tremble in horror at the very idea.

"No tears in the writer, no tears in the reader. No surprise in the writer, no surprise in the reader." — Robert Frost

There is an entire school of inspiration writing. Go ahead and Google the theme and you will find over 387,000 hits on the subject. There are numerous books, programs, quotes, articles, courses and even software that will teach you how to be an "inspirational" writer. Paradoxically, the father of writing is much less popular. When I type in Google "perspiration writing" I am only able to find 1,090 hits on the topic. Apparently sweating is much less popular as a writing motive than inspiration.

"If genius is one percent inspiration and ninety-nine percent perspiration, then as a culture we tend to lionize the one percent." — Susan Cain

When I wrote my blogs on immigration, I read over a dozen books on the subject before I started to write. I read pro-immigration books, anti-immigration books, history of immigration books and some textbooks on immigration law. The result of this research was a three-part series on immigration. I am proud of this work. I put a lot of time and effort into the writing in the hope that it would reflect an intelligent and actionable manuscript. I wanted to produce a piece of writing that might help people who were thinking about immigration policy and not sure what we should do about it. I created a t-shirt that read: "Necesitamos una política migratoria justa. No una política anti-inmigración." Translated, it means "We need a fair immigration policy. Not an anti-immigration policy." I hoped to express an opinion that would be shared by other people in Arizona where I live in the winter. (See my blog titled: **"My Take on Immigration"**

There are those who would say that writing must be comprised of both inspiration and perspiration. Writing they say is 99 percent perspiration and 1 percent inspiration. Such formulas are more easily quoted than done. Many the author who has had a brilliant idea and then waited years for another spark of brilliance. The great science fiction writer Ray Bradbury wrote at least 27 novels and more than 600 short stories and yet is primarily remembered for one novel: Fahrenheit 451. It is rare indeed for many scribes to be remembered for even one. There is a large degree of serendipity that goes into any popularity that does not seem to be captured by effort alone. Think of all the books that were written on the O. J. Simpson Trial. There were over 7.000 books dealing with various aspects of this case. How many of them can you name or remember? One might argue that most if not all of these tomes were written based on the sordid idea of making money. Whether any of them were guided by pure inspiration is a question that probably cannot be answered. Nevertheless, there is little evidence that even adding inspiration will make a successful book. The Goddess of Success seems to be fickle when it comes to writing.

"The moral flabbiness born of the exclusive worship of the bitch-goddess SUCCESS. That – with the squalid cash interpretation put on the word 'success' – is our national disease." — William James

You and I may never be a Hemingway or a Faulkner or a Stein or ever write a "best seller." What really matters is that we share our joys and fears with the world and bring passion and conviction to our effort. If we can do this, then the question of inspiration or perspiration will fade away like Mac Arthur's "Old Soldiers."

Time for Questions:

Have you ever wanted to write something? When will you start? Did you write today? Why not? What is holding you back?

The End

Hope you enjoyed my stories. I am working on Volume 2. If you have any ideas for stories or would like to comment on any of these, my email is persico.john@gmail.com

I am a semi-retired educator and management consultant who loves exercising, traveling, dining out, music, meeting new people and most of all, reading a good book.